ASK YOUR
FATHER

First published in Great Britain in 2005 by Robson Books, The
Chrysalis Building, London W10 6SP

An imprint of Chrysalis Books Group plc

First published in 2004 by Gusto Company AS
Copyright © 2004, 2005 Gusto Company AS

The right of Michael Powell to be identified as the author of
this work has been asserted by him in accordance with the
Copyright, Designs and Patents Act 1998.

The author has made every reasonable effort to contact
all copyright holders. Any errors that have occured are
inadvertent and anyone who for any reason has not been
contacted is invited to write to the publishers so that a full
acknowledgement may be made in subsequent editions of
this work.

British Library Cataloguing in Publication Data
A catalogue record for this book is available from the
British Library

1 86105 860 8

Original concept by James Tavendale and Ernesto Gremese
Illustrated by Greg Paprocki, Artville and Photodisc
Original design by Bulle Visjon
Original cover design by SEE Design
Printed by SNP Leefung, China

Fifty Things Your
Father Should Have Taught You
But Probably Didn't

ASK YOUR
FATHER
By Michael Powell

Introduction

I am eight years old and I am watching my father mow the lawn. He is wearing his gardening clothes: a baggy thick-knit jumper with holes in the elbows, an old pair of trousers and large white woollen socks which are folded over the top of his wellington boots. The cold air is sweet and crisp with the smell of grass clippings.

The volume of the engine ebbs and flows as he cheerfully glides from one side of the lawn to the other, pausing now and then to flick away a fir cone or other small obstacle that might damage the blade.

Occasionally he looks up and smiles at me above the noise. I want to ask him a question, but I sit silently for several minutes until finally he switches off the engine.

'Dad. How old will I be before I can mow the lawn?' It is a question I must have asked many times before. Today he turns the handle of his Flymo towards me, raises his eyebrows slightly and replies, 'How about right now.'

Standing behind me, he pulls briskly on the starting cord and the engine roars into life once again. I feel trusted and loved and very grown-up. Vibrations buzz down my arms as, gripping the handle together, we begin a silent two-step.

Our fathers teach us how to be men by example; it is our choice whether to follow. My father was also in the habit of stripping down to his swimming trunks and climbing in to the septic tank whenever it needed cleaning. I don't recall ever asking if I could help.

But nobody can know everything – even if they are your dad – which is why I have written this book, containing fifty things your father would teach you if he knew it all, (or if you had the guts to ask him).

My father is a quiet, gentle and intelligent man who has helped me more than I can know, but he didn't teach me everything in this book (for example, I haven't a clue whether he has ever been inside a strip club, or knows how to unclasp a bra with one hand), but I am grateful for growing up knowing that whenever I asked a question, I could always rely on him to patiently offer me his best explanation.

Now I have a son of my own who will be eight next birthday. He watches in awe whenever I mow the lawn. The time is fast approaching when I shall invite him to dance with me just like I did with my own father one autumn afternoon many years ago.

I hope I will always answer my son's questions with my father's calm patience. Maybe when he is older he will discover this book on a high shelf, blow away the dust and realise that his old man knew a thing or two after all.

Michael Powell

Contents

**Etiquette
requires us to admire
the human race.**
MARK TWAIN

CHAPTER 1

Style

and
Etiquette

How to Be a Gentleman

Where have all the gentlemen gone? It's seems impossible to walk down a street today without seeing guys slouching, losing their temper, swearing and blinging. Yet, good breeding, style and taste are qualities that are as important today as they have always been for men who wish to make their mark and rise to the top.

1. Always be polite.
2. Do not swear.
3. Keep your cool.
4. Wait until everyone else is seated before you start eating.
5. Give up your seat to others on public transport.
6. Light a match or open a window after you go number twos.
7. Never talk about how much you earn, unless you are asking your boss for a raise.
8. Only take as many condiment sachets as you intend to use.
9. Show up on time.
10. Never throw cigarette butts from a moving vehicle.
11. Do not pick beer mats apart.
12. Only wear sweats in public if you're jogging or in the gym.
13. Do not rubberneck at road accidents.
14. Do not wear your keys on a chain.
15. Make sure your belt matches your shoes.

#

Do not overfill your salad bowl at a pizza restaurant.

16. Do not repeatedly press your pecs to see how firm they are.
17. Trim your fingernails and keep them clean.
18. Do not cut holes in your trouser pockets.
19. Use aftershave sparingly.
20. Do not overfill your salad bowl at a pizza restaurant.
21. Never pay for sex.
22. Do not pretend to know more about slot machines than you really do.
23. Only be the first to sit down at a dinner table if you are invited.
24. Do not keep cigarettes or pens behind your ear.
25. Scoop the spoon away from you when you are eating soup.
26. Keep your mobile phone out of sight.
27. Do not jangle your loose change.
28. Always keep your word.
29. Do not make room when you break wind.
30. Never drink beer at a bus stop.
31. Do not torture your pets.
32. Always offer to pay.
33. Do not wear cartoon character ties or waistcoats.
34. Walk away from a fight.
35. Do not run with scissors or use them to pick your ears.
36. Always walk between a woman and the road.
37. Break bread rolls into pieces rather than stuffing the whole thing into your mouth.
38. Do not pick your nose at traffic lights.
39. Learn how to slow dance.
40. Always stand when a woman or your superior enters or exits the room.

How to Shave Properly

It's only in the movies that a man can get a close shave by covering the bottom half of his face with foam then immediately wiping it off again with a towel to answer the phone or a knock at the door. In real life, guys, you actually have to use a razor.

Purchase some average-priced disposable ones. If you're the kind of person who buys your socks, shirts and shaving products in packs of fifty, you're probably wondering why your face looks like a chorizo and you're not getting any action. But neither should you believe those ads which suggest that the best way to encourage beautiful woman to stroke your chin is to employ top-of-the-range four-blader technology. They're just razors, not global positioning systems.

Use a single blade if you have more than four days' growth, since the hairs will get trapped between twin or triple blades even when you shake the razor underwater. You'll have to use a scrubbing brush to get them out (maybe manufacturers hope you'll waste razors this way).

Shave immediately after you've had a bath or shower when your bristles are softer and easier to cut. Also, use a shaving cream instead of foam as it will leave your skin more moistened.

Take your time. If you rush you'll end up with razor burn (also known as Physics Teacher Rash).

#

Shave immediately after you've had a bath or shower.

For a closer shave, pull the skin tightly upwards then shave downwards slowly in the direction that the hair grows

There are two schools of thought on which bits to shave first. Some argue that you should start on your cheeks to allow time for the harder bits to absorb moisture from the shaving cream and become softer; others suggest cutting the tricky bits first when the blade is at its sharpest – although this has the disadvantage of making the blade blunt quicker, as these hairs will be harder. A man's life is full of tough choices.

For a closer shave, pull the skin tightly upwards then shave downwards slowly in the direction that the hair grows (going with the grain). Only shave upwards occasionally for a really close shave, as it can strip away a lot of skin (analysis of shaving remains shows that we take off as much skin as hair).

After your shave press a hot damp towel on your face to open the pores, then rinse with cold water to close them again. Finish off with a moisturiser.

And don't leave hairs in the sink, you slob. It doesn't take much to rinse them away. Bin the razor, unless you like storing bacteria and blood products in your bathroom cabinet. You'll appreciate being able to use a fresh one next time instead of last week's leftovers.

#

After your shave press a hot damp towel on your face to open the pores.

Make a Great First Impression

It is a cliché that first impressions count, but they also last and build. An inept introduction can lead to an awkward second meeting and so on. It is also true that the first twenty seconds are vitally important. Human beings like to classify and categorise, so you need to concentrate on attaching positive associations to yourself from the outset.

If you hate such stiff conventions, bear in mind that an elaborate social game it may be, but it's a game that everyone else is too busy playing to care what you think about the rules. If you don't take part then you're left standing on the sidelines. Is that what you want? Appearances matter. All of the things that you want in life will be achieved with greater ease if you learn how to follow a few social rules.

The handshake

Always stand up to greet people. Insecure people often remain seated because they dislike the formality associated with standing up, but it makes them appear disinterested, clumsy and socially inept.

Look the other person in the eye, smile and grip their hand firmly, making sure that the crook of your finger and thumb meets theirs. Shake cleanly up and down once and say 'Pleased to meet you'.

LOOK THE OTHER PERSON IN THE EYE, SMILE AND GRIP THEIR HAND FIRMLY.

Then release, while maintaining eye contact. Pay attention to their name. It's easy to concentrate so hard on creating the right impression that you forget to listen.

The Three Vs

These are Visual (your appearance), Verbal (what you say) and Vocal (how you say it).

Visual

This accounts for over half of the impression you create. It goes without saying that you should be well-groomed, but your appearance should also be appropriate. If you want to succeed then you will get further by conforming to the norm within your chosen field than building a reputation as the guy with the wacky hair or Mickey Mouse waistcoats. Even so-called non-conformists like pop stars work very hard to look like pop stars! In your efforts to be individual, you will probably just end up being 'different'. Others may well compliment you on your appearance, but it could put up more barriers than it breaks down.

But there's more to your appearance than your clothes. Your body language will give you away no matter how you dress. Smiling, good posture and maintaining eye contact are paramount. Try to keep as still as you can without becoming stiff. Stillness conveys calmness and confidence and also makes you more approachable.

How does your body behave when you are nervous? Some people fold their arms, while others jangle change in their pockets, fidget, puff out their chests, cover their mouth or play with their hair. Recognising your own mannerisms is the first step to consciously stopping them.

Vocal

How you speak accounts for about a third of the impression you create. Speak clearly at a moderate pace and try to recognise how stress affects your voice. Some people raise the pitch or tempo, while others talk in a monotone because they may be trying to appear serious or reliable. We all do something, so learn how nerves affect you and try to understand the reasons why.

Verbal

It may be a relief to learn that less than one tenth of the impression you create comes from what you say. So concentrate on making the other person the centre of attention and being a good listener. Ask open questions that keep the conversation flowing. Use his/her name frequently (but don't overdo it).

Always try to find common ground and interests and don't feel that you have to talk 'business' all the time. In some cultures it is unthinkable to mention business until several meetings have taken place.

How to Tie a Tie

A Chinese philosopher once said that a tie strangles clear thinking. Certainly, the leaders of the Dot-com revolution didn't seem to own a tie between them. However, even if you do subscribe to geek chic and business casual, you should still have a few nifty knots at your disposal for those occasions when you are obliged to place one of those little silk nooses around your neck.

Four-in-Hand Knot

This is the basic knot that many men know, but it is not the most symmetrical and is quite thin.

1. Button up your collar and flip it up. Place the tie around your neck with the wide part (X) hanging 30cm below the thin part (Y).
2. Wrap X around Y once and slip it up through the loop.
3. Tuck X down through the knot.
4. Pull Y to tighten the knot.
5. Hold Y with one hand as you slide the knot up to your neck with the other.

Half Windsor

This is a thicker, more symmetrical knot, which requires a long tie.

1. Button up your collar and flip it up. Place the tie around your neck with the wide part (X) hanging 30cm below the thin part (Y).
2. Wrap X over Y then bring it towards you

down through the loop.

3. You should now have a little triangle with the back of the wide end lying behind the thin end. Going from left to right, wrap X around the triangle then bring up through the loop.

4. Feed X down through the knot.

5. Hold Y with one hand as you slide the knot up to your neck with the other.

The Full Windsor

This is a very thick symmetrical knot which requires a very long tie.

1. Button up your collar and flip it up. Place the tie around your neck with the wide part (X) hanging 30cm below the thin part (Y).

2. Pass X over Y then bring it up through the loop.

3. Pull X over the right of the neck loop.

4. Wrap X around the back of the knot and bring it towards you down over the left side of the neck loop.

5. Wrap X around the front of the knot and bring it up through the centre of the loop.

6. Tuck X into the front of the knot and then pull down.

7. Hold Y with one hand as you slide the knot up to your neck with the other.

Mobile Phone Etiquette

Are you a cell savvy user or an annoying pest? Are you sensitive to those around you or do their hackles rise every time your Eminem ringtone blares out of your pocket? Even if you're a mobile addict, here are ten rules that every guy should follow.

1. Never use your mobile while driving. Studies have shown that you are four times more likely to be involved in an accident while using a mobile, even a handsfree set. Even if you don't crash, your ability to make driving decisions is impaired while vital brain space is dedicated to talking. Remember how your computer slows down when you try to do too many things at once? It's the same with your brain.

2. Most people think they are sensible and polite users. Most people are not. Everyone thinks the rules don't apply to them. For example, 63% of motorists in recent research reported 'frequently' seeing other drivers behaving carelessly while using a mobile phone, while only 4% admitted to regularly using one while driving.

3. Speak as quietly as you can. If there is any interference on the line, call again to get a better connection, so you don't have to shout.

4. Switch off your mobile when you are in a meeting, in libraries, theatres, museums,

restaurants, places of worship and enclosed public spaces such as toilets, lifts or buses. If you can't maintain at least a five-metre exclusion zone around yourself, don't make or take the call.

5. Switch to vibrate most of the time – it's much easier to recognise a vibrating pocket than a ringtone.

6. Keep your ringtone simple and discreet. Only teenagers will be impressed by your invasive phat tonez, or they might just think you're a bit sad.

#

Most people think they are sensible and polite users. Most people are not.

7. If you are sitting next to someone, say on a bus, and you start speaking on your mobile, it invades their personal space. It's as if they have ceased to exist and their seat has been filled with the person you are talking to. Don't do it.

8. Don't air your dirty laundry in public. If you want to row with your girlfriend or find out who your mate shagged last night, wait until you are in more private surroundings.

9. If you are with someone and your mobile rings, let it go to voicemail and check the message later. It's really flattering when you give preference to those you are with in person, rather than a disembodied voice in your ear.

10. You've just got the latest model and you want to show it off – so put it in your pocket and wait for it to ring. Keeping your mobile on display – on a tabletop or carrying it in your hand – is just embarrassing.

Choosing Wine at a Restaurant

Do you break into a cold sweat when it's time to order the wine at a smart restaurant? Do you always end up playing safe by choosing a medium-priced bottle? Which colour should you choose – cheap or expensive, full-bodied or light and crisp? What are the rules?

Wine is like sex in that most men don't like to admit they know little about it, but really, there's only one rule: choose what you like and trust your own tastes.

Everyone experiences the sights, sounds and tastes of the world in their own unique way so, at the end of the day, a wine 'expert' who knows a lot about wine is still talking about his own preference, which is bound to differ from yours. That said, if you always stick to a couple of wines that you like, you could be missing out on making lots of other great wines your personal favourites. Don't be afraid to ask the wine waiter for a recommendation.

It helps to know about wine and what you like, but that doesn't mean you have to stick to any 'rules'. In the old days, the idea about having white wine with fish and red with meat was more applicable because then whites were lighter, whereas now some whites – like barrel-aged

Chardonnay or Gewurztraminer – have more body than a Pinot Noir or Beaujolais.

So, forget about colour and think instead about 'how big the taste is'. If your food is rich and hearty (beef, game, cheese, lamb) you should choose a full-bodied wine, otherwise you won't be able to taste it. However, if your meal is lighter (chicken, fish, pork, sea food) you can choose anything you like. Purists insist that a strong wine will destroy the delicate flavours of a subtle dish, but if you like strong wine, then drink it, rather than choose a bland little Soave that leaves you unsatisfied.

Is an expensive wine really worth its hefty price tag? It's hard to believe that a bottle costing £1,000 can taste 200 times better than one that sets you back a fiver. Again, it's all a question of taste.

Spend whatever it takes to more than satisfy your palate. If you don't like the taste of cheaper wine, don't buy it. Most people do notice a difference between a cheap and middle-priced wine, but if you're not one of them, don't lose sleep over it but neither should you limit your choices.

So trust yourself, always be open to new experiences and never, ever, try to bluff.

Ironing Your Clothes

Ironing is men's work. That's why it forms such an important part of army training. The first thing a soldier does when he is deployed in a combat situation is to secure the laundry facilities. So if you want to dress to kill (even if you don't actually want to be a trained killer), you should still know how to get the best out of at least two items of clothing: your shirt and trousers.

SHIRT

1. Read the label for instructions on ironing temperature.
2. For best results, iron when your shirt is still a little damp. If using a steam iron, fill it with distilled water to avoid clogging.
3. Undo all the buttons.
4. Iron the back of the collar from the outer points to the centre, then repeat on the front.
5. 'Dress' the ironing board with the shirt face down. Then iron the shoulders or 'yoke'.
6. Sleeves: iron with seams on top of each other, then with seams parallel. Do not put in a crease. You want to end up with a smooth cylinder with no crease.
7. Cuffs: inside first, then outside, holding them taut so that they don't wrinkle.
8. Finally, iron the right front panel, pressing in between the buttons, then rotate to iron the back (press side seams from inside then outside), then the left front panel.

Do not iron stained or dirty clothes as this will fix the stain or dirt into the fabric.

9. Put on a hanger (do up the collar and top two buttons to keep the shape) and allow to cool before wearing, otherwise it will crease again.

TROUSERS

1. First turn your trousers inside out and iron the waistband, pocket linings, crotch and cuffs.
2. Turn them the right side out again.
3. If ironing black trousers, don't iron the fabric directly, but place a damp white cloth over it, otherwise you may get shiny patches.
4. Place one leg down the length of the ironing board and iron flat from top to bottom. Make sure you iron along the existing crease. Then turn over and press the inside leg. Repeat with the other leg. Don't press both legs together, or you will create multiple creases.
5. Rub soap or wax into the inside of the creases to keep them for longer, the old-fashioned way.
6. Hang your trousers up immediately and allow to cool before wearing. Do not iron stained or dirty clothes as this will fix the stain or dirt into the fabric.

Making a Speech

If you've had little or no experience of speaking
in public, when the boss wants you to make a
presentation or your best mate asks you to speak
at his wedding, it can be a daunting prospect. But
the two most important things for a successful
speech, as with many things in life, are preparation
and relaxation.

Preparation

Prepare your speech well in advance and try to
familiarise yourself with it. Even if you are reading
directly from a manuscript, your aim is still to
speak as though you are thinking the words for
the first time.

Allow time for the thoughts to appear in your mind
before you speak them. Don't feel that you have to
memorise your speech. A written speech presented
with sparkle and spontaneity is preferable to one
where all you can think about is trying to
remember your lines.

Develop a conversational style. Public speaking is
still speaking – and you've been doing that for
years. Involve the audience as you would if you
were speaking to a single friend. The other thing
you do in natural speech is look at the person you
are talking to – it's no different whether you're
speaking to one or one thousand. Make plenty of
eye contact.

Vary the speed, volume and pitch of your voice. Nobody wants to listen to someone speaking in a monotone.

Use your body: gestures and movement. It's what you do when you're speaking to your friends; so don't clamp your arms to your sides just because you're in front of an audience.

Let your emotions arise spontaneously as you speak, but don't force them. If you are relaxed, you will be able to tap into the same emotions that you express so easily in everyday conversation.

Good acting consists of conveying believable human characteristics and emotions, and it's the same with public speaking. Above all, your audience wishes to experience a human being talking to them, so be natural and don't stifle your personality beneath a formal oratorical veneer.

Relaxation

The best way to relax is to centre your breathing. Nerves often make us take short shallow breaths, when what a good speaker needs is to support their breath by breathing much further down, from the stomach rather than the chest. The stomach is an emotional centre, the place where you feel butterflies, and first love and fear, so it is natural that if you can connect your breath to this area, your voice will be well supported and modulated.

Smelling the Rose

This is a great little exercise for centring your breath and calming your nerves. Imagine you're smelling the most beautiful rose in the world. Hold this imaginary flower to your nose and breathe in, allowing the delicate scent to fill your

VARY THE SPEED, VOLUME AND PITCH OF YOUR VOICE.

nostrils, sinuses and head with the glorious aroma. Then on the out breath, rub your tummy and say 'Mmmmmmm . . . yummy, yummy, yummy' really expressing the joy and delight of this wonderful smell. If you repeat this several times you will soon find that you are actually breathing from your stomach.

Wake up your body. Do something, anything that wakes and warms up your body so that you aren't just living in your head with your nerves and voice.

From a standing position, curl over and allow you arms to hang down towards your feet, then gently shimmy your shoulders while breathing into your back. If you can get someone to rub your back, even better. This will lengthen your spine and make you feel more relaxed. Then curl back up again one vertebra at a time until your head is the last thing to return to level.

Now you are ready to give your speech. Remember one last thing: Tell a story. This means knowing where you are and where you intend to go. Think of a speech as an opportunity to take both you and your audience on an exciting journey and enjoy the ride.

How to Ask for a Raise

Asking for a raise can be nerve-wracking, even when you deserve it. Just realise that asking is better than not asking, whatever the outcome.

Be confident. If you don't believe that you deserve a raise, why should your boss? Bosses love to see results, so spend some time thinking about specific results you have achieved that support your case. It is much harder to say no to someone who can list twenty ways in which they have excelled above the call of duty or brought value to the company.

Choose your timing carefully. There's no point asking for a raise when you've just screwed up, or when six of your colleagues have just been made redundant. Ideally, you've been building a good relationship with your boss and others within the company for several months or years.

#

Choose your timing carefully.

Know what you are worth within your industry. If you ask for an unrealistic amount you will lose all credibility. Ask around friends in other companies and look on the Internet for salary surveys, or check the classifieds for equivalent jobs to see what salaries are being offered.

Don't just think about money. There are lots of other ways of improving your prospects: more flexible working hours including working some

days at home, more holiday, a lap-top you can use at home, share options, etc.

If you're already at the top of your pay scale, think of extra responsibilities you can take on to justify a raise – it will make you look committed and ambitious.

Anticipate your boss's objections and think of comebacks. If your boss gives you a flat 'NO' then ask for a time scale in which s/he would be prepared to reconsider or ask for feedback on what you would need to do to qualify for a raise in the near future.

If the answer is 'No' then at least you are in a stronger position than you were before you made your feelings known. Now your boss will know that you know what you are worth and the next time you ask for a raise it won't be a surprise.

Three mistakes to avoid

Don't say why you need the extra money. It makes you sound unprofessional and is irrelevant. Focus on demonstrating your worth not your needs.

Don't let on that you know what your colleagues are earning and that you want the same or more. This is guaranteed to make you look indiscreet and will also make your boss defensive.

Don't threaten to leave unless you have a better job lined up somewhere else. You'll look disloyal and untrustworthy. If your boss really thinks you're indispensable then you'll probably have had no trouble in getting a raise by now anyway. Instead, show your boss how much you enjoy working for the company.

Smoking a Cigar

It has been said that to smoke is human; to smoke cigars is divine. In fact, it's an art form. A Cuban cigar is a wonderful thing, requiring over a hundred steps to complete. Real men are rarely seen without one and they really know how to handle those babies, too. Winston Churchill chugged his way through twenty large Havanas every day!

Nothing feels more manly than sitting in your favourite Chesterfield taking deep and dignified tokes on an expensive handmade premium cigar while you discuss politics, drink vintage cognac and commune with the spirits of Ernest Hemingway and Groucho Marx . . . but wait a moment. Did you just inhale? It looks like you need a crash course in cigar management.

Choosing a cigar

The shorter and thicker a cigar, the greater its intensity. As a novice you should choose something longer and thinner, unless you want to cough your colon out.

Squeeze the cigar slightly. There should be no lumps and the colour should be uniform. If the end of the cigar is discoloured, don't buy it.

Make sure it contains 100% tobacco (cheaper cigars are filled with all sorts of rubbish like mashed potato and sawdust). Have no truck with cheapo cigars, fit only for the recreational pursuits of presidents and interns.

Making the cut

Clint Eastwood looks really cool when he bites the end off his stogie and spits it out (usually in the direction of a stray dog), but this is neither the most effective nor sophisticated way of removing the end.

Use a single-bladed cutter to remove the head with a clean horizontal guillotine action. Cut where the cap of the cigar meets the wrapper. A double-bladed cutter will slice the cigar from both sides and increases your chances of a smooth cut that doesn't tear the wrapper.

Lighting

The care with which you light your cigar is crucial to its taste and your pleasure.

Don't use matches or a kerosene cigarette lighter, as the sulphur and ammonia will interfere with the subtle smell and taste of the cigar. Besides, most matches don't burn for long enough.

Use a butane lighter, which is odourless, or a sliver of cedar from the cigar box. Angle the cigar no more than 30° below horizontal, otherwise you will soot up the end of the cigar and affect the taste.

Rotate the cigar slowly to light the entire rim, otherwise it will burn unevenly. Then take several quick puffs. At all costs you must avoid sucking soot or chemicals into the taste equation.

Smoking

Do not inhale!

Remove the band after about ten puffs. It's needed to stop the tobacco from tearing, but once lit it is correct form to remove it.

Get your priorities right

When offered the chance to sleep with a beautiful woman or smoke an expensive Cuban, choose the latter every time.

How to Behave in the Gym

Believe it or not, there's more to gym etiquette
than humping your grunting sweating torso
around the equipment, showing off and hitting on
every woman who makes eye contact. There's a set
of rules you'd be wise to follow to avoid gaining
a reputation as the gym meathead.

First out, don't hog the machines. A gym should
be a community of people with common goals, so
sharing is important. If you're monopolising one
machine, chances are you aren't training
efficiently anyway. If you need a rest, walk away
and give someone else a turn. For cardiovascular
machines between 20 to 30 minutes is acceptable.

**Always leave
the machine
or weights
as you
would like to
find them.**

Always leave the machine or weights as you
would like to find them. Put the weights back
and wipe down the equipment with a towel (and
disinfectant, if the gym provides it). Do you enjoy
training in a pool of someone else's sweat?

Keep the noise down. It's not cool to grunt or yell
during those final few reps. You may be feeling
stoked and ready to rip those machines apart, but
save your energy for your workout, you big
freakin' ape. Also, don't drop the weights or bang
them together when adding them to a barbell.
Being noisy is the worst form of attention seeking
that's guaranteed to make you look stupid.

Only be competitive with yourself. There will
always be someone stronger or fitter than you.

DON'T ASSUME YOU ARE THE WORLD
EXPERT ON TRAINING, EVEN IF YOU ARE.

Instead of trying to beat them, get to know them and learn some of their tips. If you enjoy beating those weaker than you, what are you trying to prove?

If you're waiting to use a machine, be patient. Don't put pressure on others to finish. Likewise, if someone is waiting for you to finish, don't dawdle, but don't rush either as you'll risk injury.

Don't assume you are the world expert on training, even if you are. Only offer advice if someone asks for it or if they look like they're about to injure themselves.

Try to resist hitting on every woman that walks past. OK, it's a fact that a gym is a great 'pick-up' joint, but exercise a little discretion. Many woman are actually interested in getting fit.

And use deodorant dude! 'Nuff said.

Get the Best Table at a Restaurant

If you are accustomed to mooching into any restaurant and find yourself sitting in the best seat in the joint within five minutes, then you are either an A-list celebrity or your choice of eateries is one up from a motorway service station. Unless you're with the in-crowd, the best places are usually booked up months in advance, so you'd better stop paying for substandard fare and learn a few tricks.

Plan ahead. The earlier you make the reservation, the better. Ask for the *maître d'* in person and explain that you have chosen his restaurant for a special occasion (make one up). Pretend you have been before and were very impressed by the food and the service. You'll come across as a major player who is both polite and complimentary.

Establish that you want the evening to be perfect, then ask his advice about where you should sit. This invites him to use his expertise to help you. If you are polite and confident he will be only too willing to help someone who takes himself and others seriously.

If you are booking at the last minute, get a friend to call the restaurant acting as your 'personal assistant'. Your friend should explain that you will be flying into town, and have asked them to find

RON AND SYLVIA LOVED PRACTISING RESTAURANT ETIQUETTE AT HOME.

the best restaurant. This raises your status and flatters the *maître d'*. He'll be falling over himself to welcome such an important customer.

Be sure to confirm the reservation before you arrive. There's nothing worse than making your party wait with you in the queue for losers.

Dress to kill and be confident, not arrogant – there's nothing more certain to get you poor service. You want to show that you deserve to be treated with respect, but that you show respect to others, as well. If you were running a restaurant, who would you put in the best seats to show off to your other customers: personable high-status individuals or arrogant bums? First impressions make the difference between being showcased at the best table or hidden behind a large floral arrangement next to the toilets.

Get your face known. Turn up on time and then introduce yourself to the *maître d'*. Shake his hand and explain who you are. At the end of the evening, thank him in person for an excellent meal. Next time he will remember you and give you even better service . . .

How to Tip Properly

The word 'tip' was originally an acronym that stood for 'to insure promptness (or politeness)'. But it's more than a crude form of insurance. It can often feel like an obligation but it helps to remember that above all it's a gift that demonstrates your generosity and appreciation of excellent service.

Now, you may think service providers should do their best without taking a 'bribe' but, if you're wondering why the waiter in your favourite restaurant doesn't seem as attentive to your every need of late, are you certain you always tip appropriately?

If you are travelling abroad, find out what is appropriate for the country you are visiting.

• In a restaurant you should tip the waiter 15% of the total bill and the maitre d' 5–10%.

• You should always leave a bigger tip when you are part of a large group (seven or more) or if you stayed for a very long time. Waiters make a large proportion of their income from tips, so if you hog a table all night, they lose out.

• If the food wasn't up to scratch, but the service was excellent, don't penalise the waiter because the chef isn't up to par. He delivers the food, he doesn't cook it!

• You should tip taxi drivers 10% of the fare and don't forget bartenders, washroom attendants, coat check attendants and hotel staff.

• You should always tip the person who carries your suitcases or shows you to your room as well as room service.

• If you are travelling abroad, find out what is appropriate for the country you are visiting. For example, in the US you should tip the bellhop $1–2 per piece of luggage or $5 for showing you to your room, even if you have no luggage.

• It is also customary in the US to tip the pizza delivery person or gas station attendant $1–2, but this is less common in the UK and other parts of Europe.

If in doubt, tip! It's better to be generous than wonder whether you did the right thing. You will look more clumsy by not tipping than tipping too much.

Buying a Suit

Every man should own a good-quality suit, even if he doesn't wear one to work. If you are unaccustomed to wearing one, that's all the more reason to be circumspect, otherwise you'll stand out a mile in your tight-fitting polyester monstrosity.

When choosing a suit, wear a shirt and tie, otherwise it won't fit properly. Then select a style that matches your height, body shape and colouring. Broadly speaking, there are three styles: British, European and American.

British
This feels very tailored and follows the contours of your body, so the shoulders have minimal padding and the waist is defined. Double vents at the back also help to define the waist but also make your bottom look bigger, so avoid this style if you have a large behind.

European

Here, the emphasis is on the shoulders and hips. The shoulders are more padded and the fit is more 'relaxed' (for example, the trousers are wider and the jacket is longer – both are unflattering for a shorter man). There are no vents, so you need a flat bottom to pull this look off.

American
This is a squarer look with a shorter jacket and no

shoulder padding. It is very relaxed and easy to wear, but if you want a 'crisp' style choose British (for example, the lapels are 'rolled' so they have a softer, less sharp edge).

Hand tailoring

A suit should be at least partially if not completely hand made and stitched. This isn't just snobbery. Hand tailoring creates a shape and cut that cannot be reproduced by a machine. For example, if the back of the collar is hand stitched it will sit better against your neck, while a collar that has been machine stitched will tend to stick out, especially when you are sitting down.

The seams should be literally 'seamless' so that the pattern or weave continues without interruption. This is especially noticeable around the pockets. Also make sure the lining is hand stitched not glued.

Trousers

When choosing trousers, bear in mind that your waist should involve your navel. Any higher and you'll look like your granddad; any lower and you'll only make the stomach you are trying to hide look even bigger. If you have short legs avoid trouser cuffs.

One hundred per cent wool

Other fabrics won't let your skin breathe properly (you'd be more comfortable and stylish wearing a bin liner than polyester) and won't hold their shape (linen creases the moment you take it off the hanger).

Choose a medium-weight wool blend, unless you are aiming for that Monarch of the Glen meets Sean Connery look, in which case you should choose tweed and buy a pipe.

#

When choosing trousers, bear in mind that your waist should involve your navel.

If women didn't exist,
all the money in the world
would have no meaning.

ARISTOTLE ONASSIS

CHAPTER 2

Women

How to Unclasp a Bra with One Hand

The best way to get good at something is to practise. If you kick a ball against a wall for long enough you may develop some soccer skills. If you shoot baskets, you'll improve your aim. But when it comes to unclasping a bra with one hand, in the dark – let's face it, how often does the average guy get the chance to hone his technique?

If you're already a make-out artist, you'll be getting lots of practice and the chances are you're probably already quite adept, but what about the rest of us, who only occasionally find ourselves in a situation where a puppy-freeing scenario looks a greater than remote possibility? If you're too shy even to approach a woman, then ask your granny if she'll let you practise on her. Or, then again, don't.

With the palm of your hand on her back, slide your middle finger under the clasp at the back of the bra strap. Pull it away from her slightly to allow you to pinch the strap between your thumb and ring finger. Beware! If at this point you make a mistake and let go, she may offer to do it herself (making you feel a confusing mixture of shame and anticipation), but chances are she'll think you pinged her strap to be funny and she'll start looking in the direction of her coat.

Remove your middle finger and snap your fingers (you could clear your throat noisily or lick her ear at this moment to muffle the noise). Snap twice for a bra which has two clasps.

Congratulations. Now it's time to warm your hands with a little structural engineering . . .

All About Foreplay

There's an old-fashioned saying that foreplay is an obligation which leads to gratification. A duty to be performed, briefly and ritualistically, to beguile a woman into letting you put another notch in your bedpost.

Hmmm. With that attitude, is it any wonder you don't know whether you're coming or . . . not coming? Admit it: she has you begging for it every night. You've tried seducing her mind as well as her body; you've cooked her dinner and rented a chick flick to get her in the mood; in fact you've pussied around the house all week, putting her needs before yours, hoping that one night she'll toss you some scraps.

Guys, it's time to reclaim foreplay as your own. It's not an IOU. You don't owe it to anyone but yourself to be a sex god in the bedroom. Why? Because foreplay is a frame of mind. And it should begin the moment you open your eyes in the morning and reach down to scratch your privates.

But we're not talking about seducing your woman all day. Here's something much more irresistible. The secret to satisfying sex is to do just one thing: forget all about it so that you can rediscover what's really lacking in your life: your sense of adventure.

Rule #1: Forget sex and seek adventure

Rule #1: Forget sex and seek adventure

Women are attracted to men who seek adventure rather than sex. Seek it and you will attract more sex than you can shake your libido at.

Rule #2: Foreplay equals communication

The moment you stop being a spectator and become a communicator and invite her along for the ride, you're being proactive and that drives women wild.

Rule #3: Come into her world

She's a very important part of your life, otherwise what the hell are you doing with her? So, make yourself an indispensable part of hers. Talk to her, goddammit; find out what she likes, needs and wants. Constantly surprise her. Get inside her head, her heart and her clothes, in that order.

Rule #4: It's all play

Aren't you fed up with conventional advice about foreplay? About kissing and undressing and all the physical aspects. Yeah, sure – kiss her everywhere. Use your lips, tongue and teeth to explore her whole body and show her what a fantastic body it is too . . . but it won't mean much if you've given up on being a frontiersman!

Get the message? Don't limit foreplay to those few fleeting minutes in the bedroom. Unless, that is, you actually want to turn into your dad . . .

#

Get inside her head, her heart and her clothes, in that order.

How to Kiss Creatively

It was Mae West who said 'Few men know how to kiss well; fortunately, I've always had time to teach them.' Being a creative kisser is harder than it seems. It's too easy to develop an automatic smooching style that sticks with you all your life and stops you from experiencing each kiss as the unique sensuous moment that it deserves to be.

Remember your first kiss? Bet your life you didn't take that one for granted. Try to find that 'Oh-my-God-we're-actually-kissing' feeling every time, even if you have been with your partner f or years. Statistics indicate you will spend about four hundred hours kissing in your lifetime, but remember that it's still an intimate act, even when it's with the same person.

Pay attention to the way that she kisses you – it's a good indicator of how she would like to be treated. If she throws you against a wall and starts sucking face, you'd come off a little weak if all you could muster was a peck on the cheek. Neither should you jump down her throat when she is expecting subtlety.

Kiss her with your whole body. Use your hands to hold her and take your time. Treat your kiss like a dance, with varying tempo, rhythm and expression, but basically let go and see where your feelings take you. If you're thinking too hard then your brain will create an over-choreographed performance that leaves her feeling manipulated. On the other hand, if you whack your tongue around like a sea otter in a sewer, she'll quickly get the message that you are insensitive and immature.

Never ask a woman if you can kiss her. It's creepy and brain-led. Let your intuition and emotions tell you when the time is right. If you're in doubt about whether you should kiss a beautiful woman, always give her the benefit of the doubt.

Close your eyes. Have you ever kissed a woman who kept her eyes open? Makes you feel kind of insecure, doesn't it?

Never underestimate the element of surprise. Tease her: be playful and imaginative. Her whole body needs attention: kiss her cheeks, eyelids, neck, ear lobes, hands, backs of her knees, gently and lingeringly. Suck, nestle, nuzzle, lick, squeeze and stroke . . .

If snogging brings out the beast in you, is it one of these?

Panda: You're a creature of habit. She knows what's coming because you never mix it up. 'Oh no, not bamboo shoots again!'

Giraffe: You've got a tongue and you're gonna use it.

Plover: You can't resist picking food out of her teeth.

Dog: Your bad breath makes her want to swoon for all the wrong reasons.

Woodpecker: You plant poky little kisses that make her feel like she's being riveted rather than seduced.

Hagfish: You always leave her covered in slime.

#

Have you ever kissed a woman who kept her eyes open? Makes you feel kind of insecure, doesn't it?

Find and Stimulate the G-Spot

Do you know the difference between a golf ball
and a woman's G-Spot?
A golfer will spend twenty minutes looking for a
golf ball.

Thirty years ago guys would consider themselves
great lovers if they could locate a clitoris.
Nowadays it's no longer a mystery, but the G-Spot
can be harder to find than a Queen Ann ottoman
at a car boot sale.

It is named after Dr Grafenberg, the man who
discovered that stimulation of this extraordinary
place can bring a woman to heights of previously
unimagined bliss. Like most pleasure zones, the
G-Spot is controversial. Some doctors believe
that it doesn't exist, while some women feel
uncomfortable having theirs messed around with.

For the believers out there: it can be found on the
back wall of the vagina between the opening and
the cervix. The most popular way to locate it is
with your fingers or penis. Before you set off
on your long voyage of discovery, resist any
urge to scurry into the garage for kneepads and
a carbide lamp.

Fingers
Getting your mitts inside a woman is one of the
most wonderfully intimate activities on earth.
Only you can judge the appropriate moment in

your lovemaking to deploy your digits, but G-spot stimulation certainly uses them to maximum effect.

With your first two fingers comfortably inside her (palm upwards and clean short nails pleeease) beckon her gently with a 'come here' movement (as if you were asking her to walk across a room towards you).

When you run into something on the vagina wall towards her belly that feels slightly ridged or like a little ball: that's the G-Spot. Keep beckoning and alternate by moving your fingers in small, slow circles, while teasing her clitoris with whatever other parts of your body are available.

Keep going until she slides screaming off the edge of the world. She may even experience ejaculation, releasing watery fluid from her urethra and soaking the bed. This is not pee, so don't get grossed out, as it may be the first time for her, too. Besides, you'll be too busy reminding her what her name is!

Penis

Boners point in all sorts of directions, but if yours curls upwards, then you've got a better chance of finding her G-Spot. If you've previously discovered it with your fingers, you should be able to send your old Adam in the right direction.

Now get in lots of practice and soon you'll easily be able to find her G-Spot, leaving plenty of time to work on your golf swing.

Impossible Questions from Women and How to Answer Them

Honesty is always the best policy, especially when it comes to relationships, but you should be on the look out for those questions that every woman knows are impossible to answer truthfully without causing offence. When you are on the receiving end of one of these five brain twisters, always give the answer she wants to hear rather than the truth.

1. What are you thinking?

Wrong: I dunno.
Wrong: I was wondering who would win in a street fight between Lennox Lewis and Annie Lennox.
Wrong: The battery is going on this remote.

Right: I was thinking how well your shoes go with your skirt and how lucky I am that you came into my life. Also I was planning how many down payments will secure us a new SUV so that we can start a large family . . .

Clue: Women always want to know that you are thinking about them and your future together.

2. Does this dress make me look fat?

Wrong: No, your fat makes you look fat.
Wrong: How far back would you like me to stand?
Wrong: You look fine, don't worry.

Right: No. In fact it makes you look skinny. My god, are those your clavicles? You've lost weight haven't you? Don't overdo it, because I love you just the way you are. In fact I'll just pop out to the shops and buy you some chocolate. You need fattening up.

Clue: Women like to feel desired, even when they look like they've been poured into their tent-sized outfits.

3. Do you love me?
Wrong: Yes, whatever love means
(aka 'The Prince Charles reply').
Wrong: Yes.
Wrong: Penalty, ref!

Right: Haven't I told you that today – I'm so sorry my darling. Of course I love you . . . more now than ever and I will love you twice as much tomorrow. If you don't mind, now I'd like to read you the poem I wrote this morning about our love, then how's about I run you a bath and cook dinner?

Clue: If a woman asks if you love her then you've already lost. You need to make her feel so loved up she never needs to ask.

4. Do you think she is prettier than me?
Wrong: Yes, but I don't fancy her or anything.
Wrong: No, but I still wouldn't mind giving her one.
Wrong: Only in the sense that she's younger and thinner . . .

Right: No.

Clue: Don't pretend the other woman is ugly. She wants to hear she is prettier than a beautiful woman, rather than be the winner by default.

Do you think she is prettier than me?

Wrong: Yes, but I don't fancy her or anything.

Wrong: No, but I still wouldn't mind giving her one.

Wrong: Only in the sense that she's younger and thinner . . .

Right: No.

5. What would you do if I died?

Wrong: I'd get over it, I suppose.
Wrong: But I like your hair just fine.
Wrong: Go travelling.

Right: I would throw myself on your coffin just as the JCB began to shovel earth into the hole. Let's not talk about it. I can feel myself filling up already . . .

Clue: Women like to feel needed.

Give a Sensual Massage

The most important quality of a sensual massage is the feeling that you both have all the time in the world. You have no expectations about where it will lead, and all your focus is on giving her pleasure and relaxation, although it can be fun to imagine making love to her while you work. She won't realise how much stress she has been carrying around until you begin to work your magic, then who knows where it could lead . . .

1. Use soft music, candles and dimmed lights to help create a sensual mood.

2. Use the best-quality massage oils that soak slowly into the skin and choose them carefully. Lavender is great for sending her to sleep, while eucalyptus or lemon grass will wake her up.

3. Rub some oil on your hands and massage the back of your own neck first. You should be relaxed when massaging someone else. If you are stressed you will be unable to understand her needs and locate the tensions in her body. This will also warm up your hands.

4. Massaging can be quite tiring both physically and mentally. Concentrate and stay relaxed so that you can massage with both intelligence and thought.

5. Start with her back, then move to her
    shoulders, arms, buttocks, thighs and calves.
    Breathe deeply while you massage and tune in
    to her breathing patterns.

6. Starting either side of the base of her spine,
    use your palms to slide up towards her
    shoulders and down again as if drawing an
    imaginary heart on her back. Splay your
    fingers on the return trip. Always massage
    either side of the spine, but never directly on it.

7. Always maintain contact with some part of her
    body, otherwise you will destroy the subtle
    rhythm of continuous touch. If your hands
    become tired, use your forearms instead.
    Maintain a consistent rhythm.

8. Use your knuckles to break down little knots
    of pressure, but do it carefully, especially
    when you are close to bone. Make little
    circular movements with your thumbs (called
    'frictions'); pinch her very gently (called
    'effleurage'); and use rapid tapping movements
    as if you are playing the piano on her back.
    Don't knead too hard or her muscles will tense
    to protect her rather than relax.

9. When you have finished with an area,
    cover it with a towel to keep her warm.

10. Talk to her and tell her much she means to
    you and how beautiful her body is.

11. Blow lightly around her neck, face, and ears
    and add a few gentle kisses as well.

12. Don't neglect her hands and feet. Apply firm

pressure to the soles of the feet and palms. End
your hand or foot massage with light kisses.

13. Give her goose bumps by running your
    fingernails against her skin.

14. Pay special attention to the area just below
    her navel. It will send tingles through her
    whole body.

15. Start off gently, then when she is warmed up
    you can apply firmer deeper pressure. End the
    whole massage with the lightest strokes of all.

TALK TO HER AND TELL HER MUCH SHE MEANS TO
YOU AND HOW BEAUTIFUL HER BODY IS.

Read a Woman's Body Language

If you want to know whether a woman is interested in you, don't try to read her mind – watch her body instead. It sends out subtle and not-so-subtle messages continually to reveal her true feelings.

Women also do lots of these things when they are ruthlessly flirting, so pay attention and see if you can spot the difference between a woman who wants you to take things further, just wants you to want to or would rather you crawled back under your rock.

Signs she's a live one

1. She gazes into your eyes or allows her eye contact to linger a little longer than normal and her pupils are dilated. She raises her eyebrows, blinks frequently and flutters her eyelashes.

2. Her legs are crossed and the top leg is pointing in your direction or she is rocking her leg back and forth in your direction.

3. She rubs her chin or touches her cheek (a sign she may be thinking about how nice it would be to have your lips brushing against them).

4. She bites or licks her lips, or touches her front teeth.

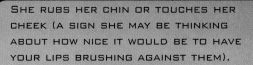

She rubs her chin or touches her cheek (a sign she may be thinking about how nice it would be to have your lips brushing against them).

5. Her face becomes flushed while she is talking to you.

6. She makes physical contact.

7. She dangles her shoe from the end of her foot.

8. She plays with her accessories or runs her fingers through her hair.

9. She rubs her wrists and exposes the underside of them to you.

10. She is smiling with her head tilted and mirrors your body language. The volume and speed of her voice matches yours.

Signs she's not interested

1. You lean towards her and she immediately backs off.

2. She turns her body away from you.

3. She won't make eye contact.

4. She doesn't touch you.

5. Her arms are folded across her chest

6. She crosses her legs at her ankles.

7. She keeps touching her nose.

8. Her hands are limp.

9. She yawns.

10. She flicks you the bird, tips her drink in your lap and leaves the room (a bit obvious, that one).

How to Be Romantic

Romance is more than making grand gestures and buying her stuff (although that scores points too). It means making your partner the focus of your attention, listening to her needs and respecting her feelings. That might make you want to hurl, but it's easier than being a selfish uncaring slob.

For example, it isn't enough to do something special on your anniversary just because that's what she expects. It's got to matter to you, too. Try getting a big kick out of the things that she likes. Guys don't really get off on receiving flowers, so it's difficult to understand why women get so hung up on them. That's because the whole world doesn't revolve around your way of seeing it.

If a guy wants a cup of coffee, he makes himself one and figures that she can make hers. That's equality right? Wrong. Women don't think like that because they are more sociable. Bringing her a cup may seem like slavery, but to her it means 'I share my life with you'.

#

Make every day a special one.

Make every day a special one. Celebrate the day you met, the day you kissed, the day you got married, her birthday; make any excuse to celebrate your togetherness. You'll soon have lots more in common than before.

Never underestimate the power of touch. That's touch, not grope. Being romantic means giving without an ulterior motive. If you think it's a short cut to getting some action . . . well you're right, but you're still coming at it from the wrong place!

Don't be a slob. This is probably the single most important thing. Did you pick your nose or forget to shave on your first date? You're dead right you didn't. So why should she find this behaviour any more attractive now?

Here are twenty great ideas for upping the romance quotient in your relationship:

1. Eat dinner by candlelight – tonight!
2. Sit through her favourite soap or chick flick on TV, even if you think it sucks ass.
3. Look at her when she's talking to you.
4. Arrange a surprise and keep it a secret.
5. Write a list of fifty things you love about her and leave it under her pillow.
6. Write 'I love you' in the condensation on the bathroom mirror while she's taking a shower.
7. Always be gentle.
8. When she comes home, stop whatever you are doing and give her a hug.
9. Praise her in front of others.
10. Compliment her appearance every day.
11. Buy her flowers or an unexpected gift.
12. Share your feelings.
13. If she is unhappy, give her a cuddle and listen.
14. Respect her opinions, especially if you disagree with them.
15. Always put her first.
16. Make her feel like she is the most special thing in your life. If she isn't, she soon will be.
17. Use your imagination. Don't leave her to come up with all the ideas.

18. Paint her toenails.
19. Go on a picnic and fly a kite together.
20. Don't take yourself so seriously.

Sit through her favourite soap or chick flick
on TV, even if you think it sucks ass.

Take time out to be totally clear and honest with yourself about what you actually want from the situation.

How to Change
a Woman's Mind

It is supposed to be a woman's prerogative to change her mind, but do you know the best method to change it for her (that doesn't involve large quantities of alcohol)?

Here's the eight-step plan to getting what you want, every time: It can be summarised as resolving conflict by communicating what you want and understanding what you are prepared to concede.

1. First of all, you must recognise that there is a conflict. (That might seem fairly obvious, when you've been arguing for half an hour and now she's packing a suitcase.)

2. Commit yourself to resolving the conflict rather than merely trying to change her mind.

3. Take time out to be totally clear and honest with yourself about what you actually want from the situation. (We often think we want one thing while actually desiring something more significant. If you know what you want, then you will be clearer about what you are prepared to concede to the other person, as concede you must.)

4. Now decide what you are prepared to accept in order to achieve a mutually beneficial resolution.

(If you think that conflicts arise in relationships only when two people want totally different things, you'll be surprised to learn that they most often appear when people are unclear about what they want or fail to communicate this effectively to the other person. When this happens, both parties resort to point scoring to 'win' the argument, rather than get what they really want. Winning an argument may give you short-term satisfaction, but does not address your long-term needs.)

5. When you are absolutely clear about what you want, you must then use three things to communicate this: logic, passion and honesty. Many men rely purely on logic. Being honest about your wants and expressing them with passion and integrity leads to clearer communication and will actually uncover more common ground and goals.

6. Focus on changing her feelings. You will always persuade people (but especially women) more with passion than logic. Advertisements change the way people think because first they change the way they feel.

7. Listen to her viewpoint and acknowledge her feelings. Separate facts from feelings.

8. Be prepared to accept your own mistakes. Admit that you don't know everything, and give up on the idea of being 'right'. This frees both of you from the burden of attaching blame.

How to Get a Woman's Telephone Number

The most important signal you should give out to become a babe magnet is that you enjoy life and you're living it to the full. It helps if you are rich and powerful with a good sense of humour, but basically this still boils down to the quality of life she thinks she's going to get if she hooks up with you.

If you are enjoying life and making those around you happy, then others will want to be part of it, including women. That doesn't mean you have to keep punching the air and saying how 'stoked' you feel. Women want substantial men, not surf bums who are too wrapped up in their own thrill-seeking to pay them any attention.

Some women are attracted to bad boys and hell raisers, it's true, but most women (apart from the dysfunctional ones who serial date crazies) look for sanity and stability; someone dependable who will be there when she needs him rather than chasing the next big wave.

Always focus on others. Don't just listen to women you find attractive; they can tell if you're faking rapt attention to get laid. Make being interested in others a habit and practise your people skills. Not only will they teach you lots, but when you meet the woman of your dreams, you'll be able to ask her some interesting questions.

Give women genuine compliments, not fake lines. Praise something about them rather than what they are wearing or their accessories.

Play to your strengths rather than focus on your weaknesses. If your pecs aren't how you'd like, forget about them. If you worry about your faults you'll forget to let your good points shine. Good salesmen never focus on the defects. Don't be too hard on yourself.

Be confident, persistent and patient. Sometimes you have to play the longer game to get the object of your desire. But don't sit back and hope your dream woman will one day appear. You've got to make it happen. And if doesn't work out, at least you tried. There's always a next time.

So how do you get a woman's phone number? Ask for it, of course.

#

Sometimes you have to play the longer game to get the object of your desire.

Cook a Romantic Meal

There's more to cooking a romantic meal than what you put on her plate, otherwise Raymond Blanc would be getting more action than Hugh Hefner. Romance is cooked up as much by the atmosphere as by simple and stress-free food. Did you get that? Simple food. You don't need Michelin stars to create an enchanted evening.

1. Plan ahead. Choose a meal which requires minimum preparation or one you can cook with your eyes closed. Cooking a complicated meal from a recipe book for the first time is stressful. Keep the food simple so you can both relax. Relaxation equals romance.

2. Dress up in something smart and sexy, and use music, candles, soft lights and great conversation, all of which are more important than the food.

3. Place no expectations on her for a night of lovemaking, though it's OK to stare at her knowingly with a flirty twinkle in your eye.

4. While you cook, run her a bath filled with sweet-smelling bubbles. Bring her a glass of champagne to sip while she soaks. When she's dressed, blindfold her and lead her to the table.

5. Candlelight. Turn off those fluorescents and get back to wax. Choose tall candles so you are both

COOK WHAT SHE LOVES AND PREPARE IT WITH LOVE.

lit from above and save the tea lights for Halloween.

6. Give her flowers at the beginning of the evening. They say 'I love you' in a much simpler way than ignoring her for two hours while you sweat over a culinary masterpiece.

7. Cook what she loves and prepare it with love. If you don't know what she likes, then shame on you. This is an homage to her, not a chance to grill yet another 16oz steak.

8. Buy really good wine. Skip the beer for one night – beer isn't romantic.

9. Prepare as many of the ingredients as you can beforehand, so the evening is spent together rather than chopping, peeling and stirring. Some of the best ingredients, such as salad dressed with extra virgin olive oil, fresh bread and fine wine, need no preparation.

10. Why not make the fire the focus of the evening. If you have a real fire in the living room, wrap a couple of jacket potatoes in tin foil and throw them in the embers, then use barbecue tongue to grill some sausages. For starters you could toast some crusty bread in front of the fire and eat with cheese and wine. The fire becomes the focal point of the evening – flickering light, primal warmth. It's slow and intimate and different, plus the flavours you get from cooking in a hearth are rich and subtle.

> As machines become
> more and more efficient
> and perfect, so it will
> become clear that
> imperfection is the
> greatness of man.
> ERNST FISCHER

CHAPTER 3

Machinery, DIY and
fixing stuff

How to Wire a Plug

Most accidents in the home are caused by faulty or incorrectly wired plugs. If your dad never taught you how to wire a plug, then shame on him, because if you get it wrong you run the risk of getting an electric shock or even burning your house down. So, unless you want hair like Marge Simpson, follow these simple instructions:

1. Remove 4 cm of outer cable (taking care not to cut through the coloured insulation on the wire strands) and you'll find three insulated wires.

2. Remove the insulation on each wire about 1cm from the end to reveal the copper strands of wire inside. Twist the strands of wire together a few times.

If you get it wrong you run the risk of getting an electric shock or even burning your house down.

3. Unscrew the big screw between the three pins and remove the plug cover.

4. Unscrew the cord grip (two screws) and set this aside.

5. Connect the brown (Live) wire to the terminal on the fuse holder marked L; connect the blue (Neutral) wire to the terminal marked N; connect the green and yellow (Earth) wire to the terminal at the top of the plug marked E. (Some appliances do not have an earth wire because they are double insulated and have no exposed metal parts.)

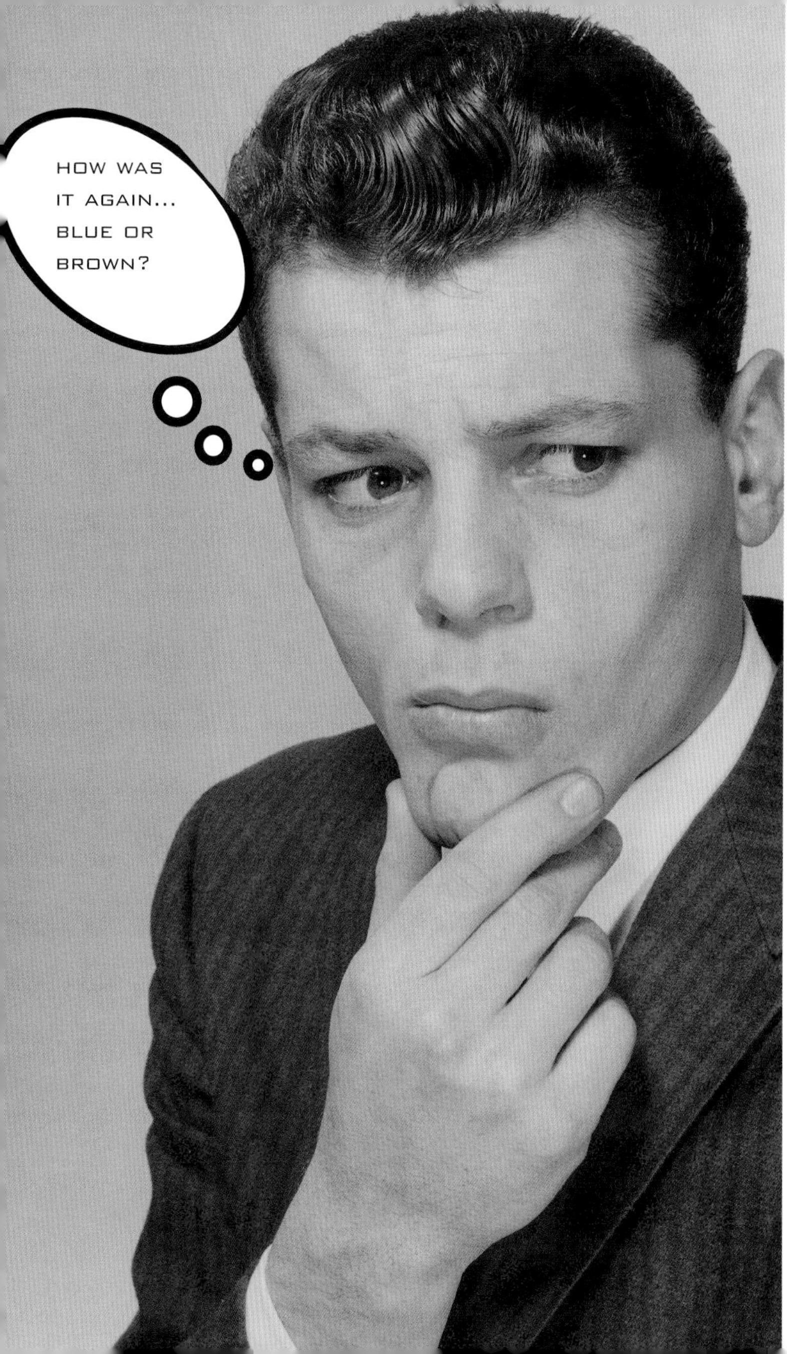
HOW WAS
IT AGAIN...
BLUE OR
BROWN?

6. Make sure that the insulation reaches up to each terminal, so there are no exposed wires (You will find that the blue and brown wires will need to be much shorter than the green and yellow wire, so make sure you cut to size first or you'll be stuffing excess wire back in place.)

7. If the plug has clamp terminals wrap each core around the appropriate terminal; place the washer on top of the twisted wire and tighten the screw nuts firmly. Make sure that the coloured insulation is not pinched under the terminal clamp. If the plug has pillar terminals, then double the twisted bare wire back on itself for about 5mm and insert it fully into the hole in the appropriate terminal. Tighten the terminal screw firmly on the wire.

8. Tightly re-screw the cord grip over the outer insulation of the flex. Make sure that the cord grip is clamped on the full outer covering of the cable and not on the inner cores.

9. Fit the correct fuse in the plug (read the instructions on your appliance to see which rating to use).

10. Replace the plug cover and, finally, tighten the big screw.

How to Paint

Painting with a professional finish is easy so long as you do things in the right order with the right tools and – most important of all – make the right preparations.

First, remove all furniture and cover the floor with a professional-quality canvas sheet. (Don't use your old bed sheets – they're too thin and any spilt paint will soak through them. Avoid plastic as it's too slippery.)

The hardest part is actually preparing the walls. You should spend longer removing surface irregularities, filling holes with filler and sanding than you do actually painting. Remove all wallpaper. Wash the walls with a mild detergent to remove dust and grease. Caulk all gaps between wall and skirting board/window/door casing with paintable caulk and smooth with a damp cloth. If you cut corners at this stage the end result will be uneven and shoddy.

Measure the area of your walls and ceiling so you know how much paint to buy. Coverage is written on the tin. Use matt emulsion for walls and ceilings, vinyl silk for areas of high humidity like bathrooms and kitchens (or children's bedrooms for ease of wiping clean) and gloss on woodwork. Buy a brush with natural bristles and a natural (lamb's wool) roller.

If you are painting fresh plaster you must use a primer, or a 3–1 paint/water mix for the first coat. If you are covering existing paint, just use primer on the exposed or filled patches. Paint from top to bottom and corners to middle: ceiling, walls, woodwork.

Ceiling

Use an 8cm (3in) brush to paint a 10cm strip around the edge where the ceiling meets the wall. This is called 'cutting-in'. Then use a long-handled roller for the remainder.

Walls and woodwork

When the ceiling is completely dry, use a brush to 'cut-in' to corners, ceiling lines and areas adjacent to woodwork. Paint one entire wall or area at a time in square-sized sections and while the cut-in is still wet, to avoid an uneven finish.

Tips

If you spill paint, wipe it off immediately. It will be much more difficult to remove when dry.

When using different colours, apply the light colour first and then the dark colour.

If you have to take a break for several hours or overnight, you can get away with not cleaning your brushes and rollers if you wrap them in cling film and put them in the freezer.

If using a roller, paint a zig zag (like a W with one arm missing) then go over it again with vertical strokes to fill in the gaps. Paint woodwork along the grain of the wood.

Keep the room ventilated during and after painting.

Changing a Tyre

There's only one thing worse than changing a flat tyre in the rain: having not the first clue how to do it.

1. Park your car in as safe a place as possible. Be careful of traffic and place a red warning triangle to warn other motorists.

2. Remove the spare tyre, wheelbrace and jack from the boot.

3. Remove the hubcap with a screwdriver or the end of the wheelbrace.

4. Remove all passengers from the car. Why should they stay dry when you're getting soaked to the bone?

5. Use the wheelbrace (and nut key if they are locked) to loosen the nuts (usually anti-clockwise unless the nut has an 'R' on it). Loosen those diagonally opposite each other, rather than side by side. If they are really stiff you may have to use your foot or even stamp on the wheelbrace. (Careful you don't slip and injure yourself, since by now you will be wet and muddy.)

6. Stand the jack under the car next to the wheel. Check your manual for correct placement.

7. Put the handbrake on full and put the car into first gear (or PARK on an automatic). Place a brick, wallet or other suitable obstacle under the opposite wheel to stop it moving.

8. Jack up the car until the wheel is off the ground. Remove the nuts and slide the wheel off (after placing the nuts somewhere safe and clean like inside the hubcap). Do not put any part of your body under the car as the jack might slip, which could result in serious injury.

9. Replace with the spare, and hand tighten the wheel nuts, working diagonally as before. Then lower the car and tighten the wheel nuts fully. Replace the hubcap.

Optional: Have an argument with your partner all the way home.

Tips
- Always keep a pair of gloves handy.
- If the ground is soft, place something like a solid board underneath the jack to stop it from sinking.
- Get a garage to rebalance your wheels after you have changed a tyre.

Fixing stuff

How to Hang a Door

There's a old saying: If opportunity doesn't knock, build a door. That's all very well, but do you know how to hang it, too?

If opportunity doesn't knock, build a door.

1. First decide whether your door will be hung right or left hand. A right hand door has the hinge on the right, and a left hand door has the hinge on the left.

2. Check that the door frame is completely square by measuring the diagonals, which should match. If they don't you may have to plane the edges of the door to make it fit, or use the existing door as a template.

3. You should have about a 3mm gap top and side of the door and 5mm at the foot. Make sure you have the correct hinges for the size and weight of your door (check on the instructions on the packet).

4. If you want to remove an existing door, open it and place wedges underneath to support it. Leave a screw in the top hinge until you have removed all the others, then support the door as you remove this final screw.

5. Measure the length and plane the bottom of the door to allow 5mm clearance. Stand the door in the frame and check the width by pressing the

door tight into the hinge side. If it is too wide, plane the side to fit with 3mm clearance.

6. Now that it fits, mark the position of the hinges on the door by pressing them into place on the door frame, then drawing round the other side of the hinge on the door, then use a chisel on the side of the door to check out to the thickness of the hinge.

7. If you are using a new door jamb, chisel out small recesses for the hinges about 20cm from the top and bottom, and a third in the centre if required.

8. Drill screw holes and then screw the hinges to the door. Stand the door in the frame, again using wedges for support and attach the hinge to the jamb. Make sure it swings and closes without obstruction. If not, remove and plane again where required.

9. Fit door handles and locks according to the manufacturers' instructions (as each one is slightly different).

Laying a Carpet

Sinking your toes into a new carpet is the best reward you can get for spending a few hours laying it. Laying a medium-sized carpet is reasonably straightforward, but if you have a large area that requires you to join lengths together, phone a carpet fitter.

Remove old carpet, underlay and gripper strips. Before you start you must have a smooth and level surface. If you have floorboards, knock in any nails or you could even screw sheets of hardboard over the whole floor. If you are laying carpet on concrete, it must be dry and you may decide to treat with a damp-proofing sealant.

Nail new gripper strips around the edges of the room about 6mm away from the skirting board so that you can tuck the carpet underneath. These hold the carpet taut and stop it from moving. Use masonry nails or strong glue on a concrete floor.

Wear a pair of kneepads, as you will be spending much of your time on your knees.

Next, fit good-quality underlay, which will prolong the life of your carpet and make it feel soft. The squiggly rubber side goes face down to grip the floor. Join the edges with double-sided carpet tape. Trim the underlay up to the grippers, but not over them.

Rough cut the carpet a couple of inches oversize all around; you can even lay it out in your garden and cut it there. But make absolutely certain you've measured the dimensions of your room correctly. There's no going back once you start hacking at it.

Unroll the carpet and line up one straight edge against the wall, then fix this side to the grippers. Smooth out creases and use a knee kicker to stretch the carpet all the way to the opposite wall and attach this side to its grippers.

Working from the centre of the room outwards, push out any small creases with your hands and then fix the remaining edges to their grippers.

Push the carpet into the gap between the skirting board and the gripper strips using a bolster chisel.

Trim the excess carpet with a Stanley knife, holding it at 45° to the skirting board, changing the blade frequently to avoid snags and tearing.

Tips
Wear a pair of kneepads, as you will be spending much of your time on your knees.

Wear a face mask while you work to protect yourself from volatile organic compounds (VOCs) that can be released from a new carpet. Also keep the room well ventilated for several days afterwards.

Have a Great Lawn

The best thing about snow is that it makes your lawn look as good as your neighbour's. But how do you maintain it as a thing of beauty all year round? Well, the grass is not, in fact, always greener on the other side of the fence. The grass is greenest where it is mowed, weeded, fed, watered, aerated, thatched and top dressed.

Mowing

How often and how short? This depends on the time of year and the quality of the lawn. In the summer mow to between 1 to 2.5cm weekly. You should only mow shorter and more frequently with high-quality, well-managed turf. In dry weather cut longer to avoid weakening the grass. It's all about balance. Mowing shorter prevents disease; mowing longer reduces water and feeding needs.

Weeding

Weeds are not inevitable except in a weakened lawn. They are a sign that something is wrong; lack of water, fertiliser or mowing too short. Developing a thick healthy lawn is the best way to discourage weeds. Use a selective weed killer on a warm day when the weeds are growing vigorously. Make sure you read the directions. If you use too much you'll damage the lawn. If you have a small lawn you may prefer to use a liquid week killer and apply it only on the weeds.

Feeding

Feed in early April and again in September (this time with a low nitrogen feed) to maintain grass vigour. If you don't feed you get weed.

Watering

Water your lawn if the soil becomes dry, but don't wait until the grass colour changes. Water in the evening to prevent evaporation and slow enough that it sinks in rather than running off. Half an hour once a week should be enough during dry weather. Any more and you'll encourage shallow root growth.

Aerating

The soil becomes compacted over time, especially if the lawn is walked on, preventing air from reaching the roots. If patches of your lawn refuse to grow, even with careful watering and feeding, use an aerator to punch small drainage holes.

Thatching

Thatch is a build up of dead stems and roots. If you ignore it your lawn will need more fertiliser and water and become more susceptible to disease. Mow the lawn then rake out the thatch in April and September.

Top dressing

If you've got an irregular surface, when you cut the lawn you'll also get an irregular cut, with some patches shaved bare and others hardly touched. Top dressing removes these irregularities and improves the soil, which encourages healthy roots and thick turf. Apply 3kg per m^2 of a mixture of 6 parts sharp sand and 1 part compost then smooth it in with the back of a rake.

Build a Patio

Whether you seek a calm space to relax and admire the exuberance of the natural world, a romantic spot to dine *al fresco* on those sultry summer evenings or a place to strip down your motorcycle, a patio is a wonderful feature in even the smallest of gardens.

Planning

First decide upon a stone that blends well with your house. Then work out the pattern your slabs will make on graph paper, or download a simple free computer programme from a garden centre website. There's a huge range of stone to choose from, but a fairly standard range of shapes and sizes. Below are five common patterns, using between one and three different sizes.

- Grid
- Staggered
- Basket-weave
- Random
- Roman

You can even mix different types of stone, but aim to keep things simple and easy on the eye.

When measuring the area to be paved, allow for 6–8mm gap between slabs. Mark out the area with pegs and string and double check your measurements before you start digging.

Preparing the base

You must lay a firm foundation before laying the slabs. First remove any turf and topsoil and dig down until the soil surface is about 150mm below the intended level of the patio. Paving must be 150mm below the damp-proof course.

Lay hardcore to a thickness of between 75–100mm. Follow this with a 25mm layer of sharp sand spread with a rake and level it by tamping with a length of timber. Hire a mechanical vibrator to compact each layer in turn.

Laying the slabs

Starting against a wall, lay three slabs at a time. Place a fist-sized pile of mortar (one part cement to four parts sand and just enough water to make a firm mortar) in the corners of each slab plus one in the middle. Level slabs using a rubber hammer and a spirit level. Allow a slope of 16mm per metre so that rainwater can run off onto the garden.

Do not tread on the slabs for three days until the mortar has hardened.

Filling the joints

Use a brush to fill the gaps with a dry mortar of one part cement and three parts sand. Brush away any excess and then sprinkle the patio with a very light shower of water to help the mortar set.

Et voilà! Your very own outdoor garage.

Hang Wallpaper

There are two types of men: those who can hang wallpaper and Norman Wisdom. Which one are you? Walking up a wobbly ladder carrying two metres of sticky paper and then transferring it to a wall isn't as easy as it sounds.

Preparation

The key to success, as always, is preparation. Work out how many rolls of wallpaper you need by measuring the area of the wall and dividing by 56. Then measure the height of the wall and cut strips 10cm longer than you need (or more if you have a large pattern).

Fill in holes and cracks and sand the walls until they are smooth and clean.

Turn off the electrical power and remove switch plates and plugs.

Get hanging

Draw a straight vertical line just over a roll's width away from one corner using a plumb line or spirit level. This is where you will hang your first strip of wallpaper.

Apply the glue to the back of the first strip using a paint roller or large brush and a wallpapering table, paying special attention to corners and edges.

#

The key to success, as always, is preparation.

'Book' the strip by gathering it up into a concertina and leave for about three minutes to allow the glue to soak in.

Unbook the top part of the strip and stick to the top of the wall, allowing 5cm overlap at the ceiling. Slide the paper gently to line it up with the plumb line. Use a dry brush to press the strip against the wall, then unbook and smooth the bottom half into position.

Smooth the whole strip working diagonally from the top down and centre outwards. Prick any remaining air bubbles with a pin and then smooth. Wipe off excess glue with a damp cloth and slowly trim the edges along the ceiling and skirting board with a razor knife (change the blade if the paper begins to tear).

Repeat with the second strip, and butt the edge up against the first, but do not overlap. After ten minutes use a seam roller on the seams, but don't force out the glue.

To hang around doors and windows, smooth into place first and then make diagonal cuts to allow you to smooth into the corners.

Paper over light switches and plug outlets then cut a hole slightly smaller than the cover. Replace the covers at the end.

If you have trouble lining up the pattern, you may have an uneven wall. If so, match the pattern at eye level.

Be a Better Driver

The key to becoming a better driver is anticipating and keeping away from other people's problems. That's why pessimists are safer than optimists. Always assume that everyone else in the world is incompetent and drive defensively. For example, when driving down a road lined with parked cars, assume that someone will run out in front of you. When someone is turning off the road ahead, assume that they will not manage to turn before you arrive and be prepared to slow down if necessary. Here are twelve ways to improve your driving.

1. There's no such thing as a safe car, only safe drivers. If you've got a BMW M3 that corrects driver errors, it's easy to fall into the 'I've got a safe car' trap. Your car may be able to correct some of your errors, but it has no influence on those of other people.

2. Keep your distance. This depends on the weather and other factors, but generally allow at least one car length per 10 miles per hour. So if you are travelling at 40 miles per hour you should be at least four car lengths behind the car in front.

3. Avoid unnecessary acceleration, revving or idling of the engine. Get your vehicle serviced regularly. Check your tyre pressure once a week and park in the shade. These measures will reduce your fuel consumption and your impact on the environment.

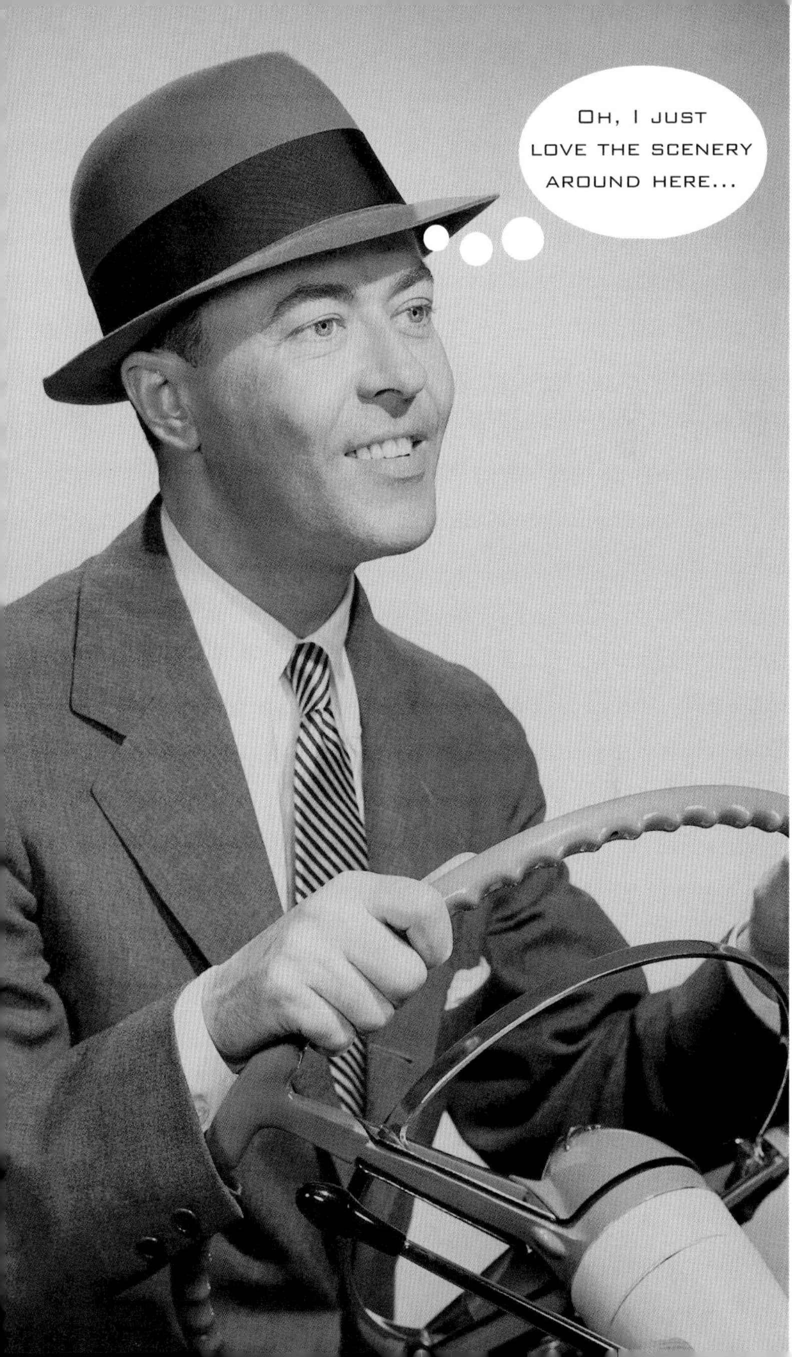
OH, I JUST
LOVE THE SCENERY
AROUND HERE...

4. Safety is not about driving, it's about attitude. Keep your cool and always try to see things from the viewpoint of other road users.

5. Avoid eye contact with other drivers who seem to be challenging or aggressive.

6. If someone is tailgating you, increase the distance between you and the car in front. This allows a greater stopping distance for you should there be an emergency, which in turn reduces your risk of being hit from behind.

7. If you know the road, you are actually more likely to crash. Studies have shown that many accidents happen close to home where people tend to concentrate less, because they are familiar with their surroundings.

8. Look far ahead. This gives you more reaction time and results in smoother steering.

9. Always try to maintain a constant speed on the motorway. Changing your speed is inefficient and may cause others to brake. The knock-on effect of your erratic driving could be a long tailback behind you.

10. Brush up on your highway code. Unless you are a driving instructor, there's lots that you have forgotten or never knew in the first place.

11. Treat speed limits as laws rather than recommendations.

12. Remember that driving smoothly requires more skill than driving fast.

Buy a Used Car

You don't have to be a car whizz to reduce your chances of driving away a turkey, so long as you are observant and use a little common sense. It is inevitable that a used car will have minor defects and problems, but you should still aim to gather as much information as you can before you part with your cash.

Here's a checklist of twenty things to look out for when buying a used car.

1. Look out for areas of rust, especially at the bottom of the bumpers, around lights, underneath doors and in the boot. If the paintwork is blistered there is often rust underneath.
2. Check for signs of repaired damage: areas where paint has been touched up or resprayed, welded seams on the floor and in the boot. If the boot or any of the doors open or close with difficulty the vehicle may have been in an accident.
3. Uneven tyre wear indicates badly balanced tyres or a damaged suspension, or even faulty wheel rotation.
4. Make sure the spare tyre is in good condition.
5. If the wheels have locking nuts, make sure you have the key or you will have to get a garage to saw off the nuts next time you need to replace a tyre.
6. Check for cracks and damage to the windscreen and windows.

7. If the exhaust pipe is blackened with soot the car may have worn rings or damaged valves, which is costly to repair.

8. Lean on the car and release; if the car continues to bounce up and down, the shock absorbers may need replacing.

9. Check the oil: if it is white or has bubbles it may indicate that water is present – a serious mechanical problem.

10. The radiator fluid should be free from rust.

11. Turn on the engine and check the transmission fluid. It should not smell bad or look dirty.

12. Test all the lights and internal electrical items like air conditioning, radio, indicators etc.

13. Check the upholstery and carpets.

14. Make sure the seat belts work and are not frayed.

15. If the car has a low mileage but many signs of wear, you should suspect that the odometer has been tampered with (the car has been 'clocked').

16. Do not buy any car without first test driving it. Listen for any unusual noises from the engine, gears and brakes.

17. Make sure the car accelerates and decelerates reliably. The brakes should feel firm.

18. Smoke coming from the exhaust is a sign of either worn valves or a cracked engine block.

19. Check the steering for responsiveness and firmness.

20. If you have any major worries about the car, arrange for it to be checked out by a mechanic. This will cost you, but it will save you money in the long run.

LEAN ON THE CAR AND RELEASE; IF THE CAR CONTINUES TO BOUNCE UP AND DOWN, THE SHOCK ABSORBERS MAY NEED REPLACING.

Jump Start a Vehicle

When your car has a flat battery, starting your
engine using the battery from another car is easy
and safe so long as you perform these instructions
in the correct order.

SAFETY FIRST
Do not jump start your engine if . . .
• The electrolyte solution inside the battery is
  frozen.
• There are cracks in the battery casing.
• The battery has been sitting for several days,
  as there may be a build-up of flammable
  hydrogen gas.

Batteries contain sulphuric acid. Wear gloves
and safety goggles at all times and if any acid
comes into contact with your eyes or skin,
wash immediately with water and seek medical
help as quickly as possible.

Do not smoke or use a naked flame during any
part of this procedure.

Step 1: Connect the vehicles
• Check the batteries are the same voltage – it is
  usually printed on the top.
• Park the booster vehicle close to the dead vehicle
  but not touching. Turn off both ignitions.
• Connect the (+) terminal (red) on your dead
  battery to the (+) terminal (red) on the booster
  battery using the positive jump lead.

- Attach the negative jump lead to the (-) terminal (black) of the booster vehicle and attach the other end to the engine block or unpainted frame of the dead car, well away from the dead battery.

Step 2: Jumping the dead battery
- Check that the cables are not in contact with any moving engine parts.
- Make sure everyone is standing well away from the engines.
- Start the engine of the dead car. If it doesn't work, wait a few seconds and try again. If it still doesn't start after thirty seconds, give up, or you'll flatten the good battery or damage the starter.

Step 3: Removing jump cables
- If the car starts, keep the engine running for at least thirty minutes to partially recharge the battery.
- You must remove the cable clips in reverse order, i.e.
1.Clip from the engine block 2. Clip from (-) terminal on battery of booster vehicle 3. Clip from (+) terminal on battery of booster vehicle 4. Clip from (+) terminal on dead battery.

Step 4: Charging the battery
- To recharge completely you should use a battery charger for at least twelve hours, because a vehicle's alternator is not designed to charge a battery which is completely flat.
- Repeated jump starts are a sign that the battery needs replacing.

Fix a Dripping Tap

Besides being torturous to listen to, did you know
that a dripping tap can waste up to 20,000 litres
of water every year? Fortunately this is a problem
that can often be fixed just by replacing the
rubber sealing washer. This is a little rubber ring
which forms a watertight seal inside the tap,
but in time it becomes degraded and worn.

#

**Fortunately
this is a
problem that
can often
be fixed just
by replacing
the rubber
sealing
washer.**

1. Turn off the water supply to the tap. The mains
   (cold) water stopcock is usually under the
   kitchen sink or outside the house; the hot water
   stopcock will be near the boiler or hot water
   tank (in the airing cupboard, if you have one).
   If you turn off hot water, be sure to turn off the
   water heating switch, so that if the hot water
   tank drains, the heater will not burn out.

2. Turn the tap on to run off excess water: any
   more than a trickle indicates you haven't turned
   the water off properly.

3. Put the plug in so you don't lose anything down
   the plug hole.

4. Remove the cap using a flat head screwdriver.
   Underneath you'll find a screw which holds the
   tap cover in place. Unscrew this and pull off the
   tap cover to reveal the brass tap stem, which is
   held in place by a large brass nut. Unscrew this

nut by turning anticlockwise with a spanner and remove the stem. Do not allow the tap spout to twist, as it may damage under-sink pipe work.

5. At the bottom of the stem you will find the old washer, or it may have broken and still be inside the tap. Remove it and fit the new washer.

6. Reassemble the tap, move it to the 'off' position and turn on the water supply.

If the tap is still leaking, then you are advised to call a plumber (like they need the work!). If the tap is leaking from the handle, you may need to replace the O-ring gasket at the top of the stem.

Tip
Every few months, turn off all taps and read the water meter. Don't use any water for a few hours then read the meter again. If the meter reading has changed, it indicates that you have a leaking tap or pipe.

A woman
simply is, but a
man must become.
Masculinity is
risky and elusive.
It is achieved by a
revolt from woman,
and it is confirmed
only by other men.

CAMILLE PAGLIA

CHAPTER 4

Being a

real man

How to Win an Arm Wrestle

If you think arm wrestling is a test of your strength, think again. With the correct technique it is possible to beat someone physically stronger than you by maximising your power of leverage.

Most amateurs lose an arm wrestle before it's even started by standing incorrectly, gripping their opponent's hand wrongly or keeping their body too far from their arm.

The Stance
Stand with your feet staggered. If you are wrestling with your right arm, place your right leg forward. If you are wrestling with your left arm, place your left leg forward.

Get a fast and explosive start.

The Grip
When you take your grip, place your index finger over your thumb. This is called 'wrapping'. This allows you to attempt a more effective toproll (see below).

Ready, steady . . . GO
Get a fast and explosive start.

Get Wrestling
When the action begins, many people make the mistake of simply exerting 'side pressure', but there's another force which you ignore at your peril. It's called 'back pressure'. This means pulling your opponent's arm away from his body

and towards your other shoulder. As long as you can keep your arm close to your body, the more power you will have to use your whole body to exert side pressure on your opponent.

Make sure that your arm and fist always stay inside your shoulders. This means using your arm and body as a single unit for maximum power.

If you successfully gain control of your opponent's hand and wrist by using 'the hook' or 'the toproll' you will usually win.

The Hook
Snap your wrist hard towards you. Now your hand is higher than his, giving you the greater leverage. Then, keeping your arm tight in to your shoulder, use your whole body to destroy him!

The Toproll
This move involves walking your fingers up your opponent's hand to gain maximum leverage while applying continuous maximum back pressure. Then pin his puny arm!

NEXT PLEASE!

Drink a Yard of Ale

Showing reckless resolve before a throng of your
baying peers by the consumption of nearly two
litres of your favourite tipple may seem like its
own reward, but there is more to drinking from
a beautifully crafted horn-shaped glass than meets
the eye.

History has flowed forward on rivers of beer –
yards of it to be precise. This gentlemanly rite of
passage has been enjoyed for centuries. There are
still yards in existence today dating from the early
seventeenth century. Their length (between 30 and
36 inches) may well have originated from their
use as a thirst-quencher for coachmen too time-
conscious to disembark.

OK, enough history. But, before you get all dewy-
eyed from standing in the shadow (or puddle) of
generations of greater men, it's worth considering
that a 'yardie' poses a stiffer challenge than
merely its ludicrous quantity of ale, namely: how
to drink in one draught without getting drenched.

Ah yes, spillage. This occurs because the ale in the
bulb tends to rush out once you've drunk the first
pint or so. You definitely don't want to go wasting
beer! Not when there are so many sober children
in Africa.

Fortunately, our forefathers have handed down
two simple techniques for the fastidious yardie.

Both methods are equally effective at mitigating the effects of an 'ale rush':

• Tilt the yard extremely slowly and smoothly.
• Rotate the glass while drinking, allowing air to reach the bulb gradually.

You should hold the neck of the glass in your weakest hand and place your other hand as far down the yard as you can reach – the longer your arms the greater control you will gain, thanks to the power of leverage.

When you have had your fill, let forth a cheery 'Whey-ha-aa-ay!' as a hearty challenge to other lionhearted fellows. Raise the glass aloft and, as you wipe your mouth with the back of your sleeve, adopt a heroic pose to demonstrate to the crowd of chanting onlookers that you truly are a leader of men.

Throw a Bachelor Party

If you're asked to be the best man at a wedding, it is your job to organise the bachelor party of the century. So come on – make it more imaginative than fifteen pints and a strip-o-gram.

You should always take your cue from the groom when it comes planning the activities. Choose something the groom enjoys. There's no point taking an inactive nerd white water rafting, or planning a trip to the ballet for an adrenaline junkie.

Also, while a little humiliation is an integral part of the day's proceedings, nothing is more important than having fun, and that includes the groom. So if you're planning to gaffer-tape him to a lamppost, do it at the end rather than the beginning of the evening. And of course, there should always be elements of reprehensible debauchery during the proceedings.

Set a date and consult with the groom. You don't want three strippers arriving at his house the same weekend his mother-in-law is coming to stay. Also hold the party at least a week before the wedding day to give everyone time to catch up on their beauty sleep and get their stomachs pumped, if required.

Plan the guest list with the groom so that he is surrounded by friends rather than people he

can't stand to be in the same room with. It's OK to have a few fun-loving chicks, so long as they aren't friends of the bride. Tell the guests how much they need to contribute and get the money up front, otherwise you'll end up maxing out your credit card to subsidise the whole bash.

It's often a good idea to have two 'levels' of fun and entertainment. The PG-rated events should happen early on, then after the groom's boss and Amish father-in-law have left, you can get on with the X-rated activities. The added advantage of having some tame stuff is you can glean a few vanilla anecdotes to tell the bride to be!

Rent a limo or private minibus to get around. This means no one has to be a designated driver and everyone is safe. Make sure the place you are travelling to is open – there's nothing worse then finding your favourite night club or go-kart racetrack boarded up for the winter after a three-hour journey and ending up in Pizza Hut.

Your final duty is to get him home in one piece at the end of the night, with or without a tattoo and his trousers. This, unfortunately, might require you to remain considerably less drunk than the rest of your party.

Get Served in a Crowded Bar

Getting a drink in a pub or club when the queue at the bar is three deep is a big downer unless you know a few tricks that will get you served quicker than the average punter.

Women get served quicker than men, even by female bar staff. If one of the barmen is obviously a playboy who likes to serve all the ladies first, then don't waste your time attracting his attention – focus on someone else.

While twenty per cent of female bar staff admitted that a nice smile helped to get punters noticed, almost all of them agreed that outright flirting would put them to the back of the queue.

Position yourself as close as you can get to the cash register, as the bar staff have to return there frequently.

Stay calm. In a recent Guinness survey of a hundred bar staff, banging the bar was behaviour least likely to get you served, while shouting, whistling, finger clicking and waving money were also likely to decrease your chances of getting served quickly.

Lean over the bar at an angle of 45°. Any less and your face will melt into the crowd; any more and you will appear too pushy. If you look too laid back they will assume you are already being served.

Make yourself appear as tall as possible. Stand on tiptoe. Tall people get served quicker than shorties. Standing next to a tall person will also get you served quicker.

Open your eyes wide and raise your eyebrows. This tells the bar staff you want serving. Make eye contact, smile and nod while pointing to your neighbour. This way you enter into an unspoken 'contract' with the bar person that s/he will find difficult to break, namely: that the person next to you should be served before you. Once you have attracted attention by your apparently selfless act, you can catch them on the return trip. Bar staff serve nice people.

Of course, the best way to get speedy service is to become a regular. This means putting in many hours of drinking every week and getting to know all the bar staff by name!

How to Host a Barbecue

A barbecue is the most important item you will ever buy (apart from maybe your car and house). The smell of charred meat stirs up visceral feelings deep within the male psyche, so it's important to be ahead of the pack if you want to thrill with your grill.

#

Keep a water spray handy to damp down any flare ups.

Purchase the biggest, flashiest barbecue you can afford: one you can cremate a whole horse on and still leave enough room for the onion rings. If you settle for anything smaller you'll feel like you're running a soup kitchen. It's really lame when every ten minutes the host shouts 'there's another burger ready' and six people are injured in the stampede. The sign of a good barbecue is when the guests are throwing sausages and ribs into the flower beds quicker than you can cook them.

Use charcoal and avoid the smug convenience of gas: you can't get in touch with your inner wild man by flicking a switch. You've got to BUILD you own fire, goddammit.

After you've lit your charcoal, let it burn for half an hour before you start cooking. The coals should be covered with a white ash. Spread them evenly over the bottom of the barby.

Cooking tips

- Precook ribs, spatchcock chickens and thick cuts of meat before lobbing them on the grill.
- Brush sauces and glazes on during the last few minutes of cooking, otherwise they will drip onto the charcoal and cause a flare up.
- Marinate your meat overnight for maximum flavour and juiciness. Fish should only be marinated for a couple of hours.
- Avoid charring the meat. Your guests will not appreciate receiving a burnt offering. The barby needs to be hot enough to seal the meat quickly, but not so hot that it burns the outside before the inside is cooked.
- Chuck a few vegetables on the barby to keep the non-meat eaters happy. But don't spare them too much thought – animals are delicious.
- Set up a table next to you with everything you need, then you won't have to keep rushing inside for stuff. This is what chefs call *mis en place*.
- Keep a water spray handy to damp down any flare ups.
- When cooking chicken, cut into the thickest part of the meat and make sure the juices run clear before serving.
- Cook fish or steam vegetables by brushing with olive oil, wrapping in tin foil and placing directly onto the charcoal.
- Stick a few of those huge garden candles in your garden to annoy the mozzies and to provide a classy ambience.
- Provide plenty of cool beer.

Check Your Testicles

It's curious how some of the names we use when referring to our testicles – nuts, family jewels – are also associated with the idea of hiding of precious items. Don't make like a squirrel. Get your nads out once a month and give them the once over.

Things can go wrong with your tackle very quickly, so it's important to get to know what's normal, so that if you spot an irregularity, you can see a doctor before it's too late.

The bad news is that testicular cancer is the most common cancer in young men between the ages of 15 and 35, affecting about 1 in 400. If you're over 35 you're not off the hook – it's just that you're now more likely to get all the other cancers! The good news is that testicular cancer is nearly always curable if you detect it early.

Examine yourself once a month to check for anything unusual. This includes lumps, pain and tenderness, discharge or pus, blood in your sperm, a heavy feeling or a build-up of fluid in the scrotum, or increase in size of a testicle.

Do the examination after a warm bath or shower, when your scrotal skin is relaxed. Place your index and middle fingers of both hands under each testicle in turn, with your thumbs on top and then roll it between fingers and thumbs. It should feel smooth. One testicle is always bigger than the other. This is normal. Also, there's a cordlike structure called the epididymis at the top and back of the testicles that carries the sperm. This is normal too!

Look out for pea-sized lumps. They are often painless, so if you do discover one, don't pass it off just because you're not in agony. Also a lump doesn't always mean cancer, but it is essential that you go to your doctor immediately.

DR MULLER'S TESTICLE HOTLINE WAS ALWAYS POPULAR...

123

TELL ME, HOW DID YOU GET THOSE ABS?
EVERYONE HAS THEM, YOU JUST HAVE TO LOSE T FAT HIDING THE

How to Get Perfect Abs

If you want to know the answer to achieving perfect abs, then you're already asking the wrong question. Do you know why? Because you already have them.

Perfect abs – *moi*? Yes. Everyone does. You were born with great abs. Do you think you don't have them now just because you can't see them? They are where they've always been: underneath all that fat that is sitting on your stomach.

When it snows, do you call the police because your car has disappeared? No, you get to work shovelling the snow away until you can see it again. If you want to uncover your abs, you need to start shovelling fat.

So, congratulate yourself on being the proud owner of a mean set of abs. What you really want to know is how to get rid of the fat, right? Which ab exercises should you do and which ab machines should you spend your money on? The answer is this: Stop whining about your abs. You're still missing the point.

Stomach exercises will strengthen your stomach muscles, which is vital for trunk stability, but without a sensible diet and exercise that makes your heart pump fast and gets you out of breath, you're wasting your time.

Get it? The only, repeat ONLY way to get a six pack is to LOSE FAT, and that means following a healthy diet and taking regular cardiovascular exercise. Isn't that fantastic news! You should be jumping for joy, because it sure is cheaper and much more fun than all those ab reps and gadgets.

But wait: doesn't isolating muscle groups help to remove fat? Says who? The guys selling ab machines? The only way to remove fat from isolated areas is the stupid lazy way: it's called liposuction.

Sure, fat likes to collect on men's stomachs and women's hips, but if you've got areas that are hard to shift, all that means is you'd like to lose more fat, not that it won't budge from certain places. Fat sits, it doesn't squat.

So, cut out the cakes and get on yer exercise bike.

WHEN MARY TOLD JIM TO GET ON HIS BIKE, HE TOOK IT LITERALLY.

How to Hold a Baby

If you're a father, or have younger siblings, nieces
or nephews, you may already be an accomplished
baby carrier. For the rest of you guys, balancing a
bambino may be something you have rarely – if
ever – done.

First of all, it won't break, although there is a
right and wrong way to hold it. A young baby's
head is king-sized, so it always needs supporting
and keeping higher than the rest of its body.
When someone hands you a baby, lean close to
them and collect it in a tight little package.

If you're at work and someone brings in their little
cherub, elbow the women out of the way and show
an interest. It's a good way to demonstrate what a
great catch you are. Better still, ask if you can
hold the baby and watch all the women crowd
around you!

There's lots of ways of cuddling a baby, apart from
at arms' length.

Cradle Hold

This is easy and the most common. The baby's
head goes in the crook of your arm, while the
other arm supports the first. Don't forget to talk
to it! 'Hello beautiful' is a great line, because it
compliments the baby and the mother. Let it grip
onto one of your fingers, or stroke its cheek. Don't

stick your fingers in its mouth. It's unhygienic and guaranteed to lose you points.

Shoulder Hold
Lean baby against your chest, supporting its bottom with the arm of the same side, and its head with the other hand. Babies love this position because they can hear your breathing and heart beat. It also enables them to puke down your back with ease.

Belly Hold
If a baby has wind, this is a great position to help relieve it. Lay the baby face down over your forearm, with your hand between its legs and use your other arm to stop it from slipping off, or rub its back gently.

Hip Hold
You would probably only use this hold on your own baby or that of a trusted friend or relative, because it can look a bit casual! Once the baby can support its own head and neck, you can sit the baby facing outwards with its bottom on one of your hips, and your arm wrapped around its waist. This leaves your other hand free to hold a beer and allows the baby to check out its surroundings.

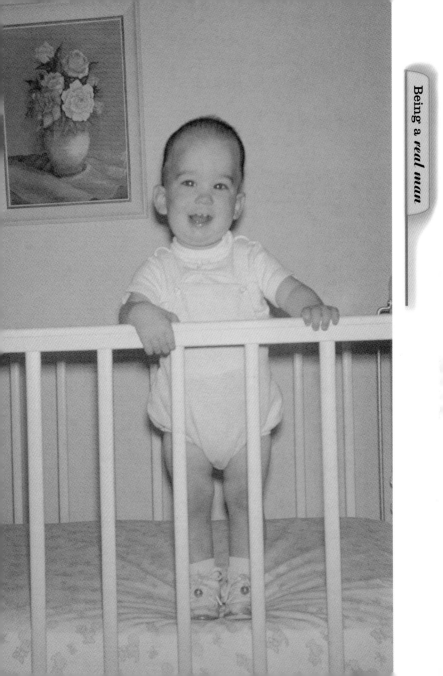

Getting a Tattoo

The first question a real man needs to ask before having a tattoo is, 'Will it hurt?' The answer is yes. Having needles piercing your skin is painful. Skin above bone is the most painful and the needles used for outlining feel sharper than the constant vibration of the shading needles.

Do you really want one? Statistically, one third of all people end up regretting their tattoo. You may want the words 'HATE' on your forehead today, but will you still be enjoying its benefits twenty years from now? Also don't get a tat of your girlfriend's name, unless you are prepared to make a lifelong commitment! Tattoo removal is expensive and difficult. If in doubt, draw a design with marker pens or buy a stick-on tat and live with it for a few weeks.

#

Statistically, one third of all people end up regretting their tattoo.

Don't get a tattoo after drinking alcohol or taking drugs. Not only will you wake up in the morning with more than you bargained for, but your blood will be thinner, making you bleed more. Even aspirin will thin your blood so avoid this too. However, you shouldn't get a tat on an empty stomach – make sure you've eaten about an hour or so before.

Even if your mate Dave offers to do it in his garage for free (known in the tattoo world as a 'scratcher'), always choose a trained professional whose work you have seen, either in a magazine, portfolio or in the flesh. You want an artist, not just a machine operator. The most common reason for regretting a tattoo is its poor quality. S/he will also follow proper safety procedures to minimise the risk of infection. Ask for a patch test to ensure you are not allergic to any of the inks.

You can choose a stock ('flash') or customised design you have made yourself (more expensive). There's heaps of choice, from intricate Celtic knotwork to full-colour, photo-realistic images. Take your time choosing and get a feel for the atmosphere in the shop. Ask questions to find out their favourite style or speciality, how long they have been in business and whether they get much custom work – all indicators of quality and stability. Make sure the place is clean and that they use disposable needles.

Remember, you get what you pay for. A good artist will charge upwards of fifty pounds per hour for custom work (less for flash). Also, if you like the work, it is customary to tip between ten to twenty per cent.

Only entrust your body to someone who makes you feel welcome, safe and is willing to give you what you want, not force their own ideas onto your skin. If the artist in any way makes you feel uncomfortable, walk away.

Avoid a Fight

The only time a fight is unavoidable is when one of the parties is a psycho who enjoys inflicting pain and suffering on others. Most people aren't – they just lose control of their emotions and try to defend their wounded pride.

Most fights start with a minor disagreement and escalate into physical aggression. Many men end up in a fight, not because they fail to spot when the situation turns nasty, but because they bone-headedly encourage it. If one party backs off, end of conflict. He might call you a pussy, but be sure that someone will whup his ass at some time in the near future. It needn't be you.

Keep your cool. If someone is provoking you, stay calm and walk away. Always walk in preference to running, as you are less likely to be followed. If you run, you will appear scared and easy prey. Walking will make the aggressor less certain about your motives.

If you're in a car and someone starts road raging, back off. Don't do anything to get him back. If you're so insecure that you need to show who's boss, then you're as big a idiot as the other guy. Let him think he's better than you. If you think you've got to be tough on the street or get walked all over, then get off the street.

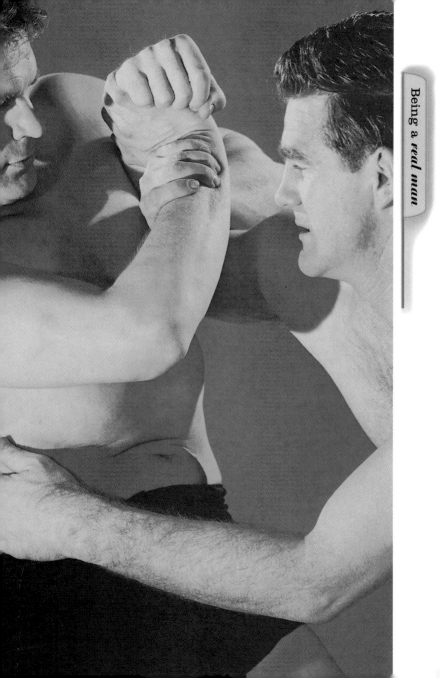

Avoid hanging around with guys who boast about the fights they've had. They're looking for trouble and they find it. You don't need to be with them when they do.

Don't drink when you're feeling low. A bad mood means your self-esteem is lower than usual. Combine this with a self-control killer like alcohol and you increase your need to prove yourself, which is a recipe for violence.

Always treat women, all women, with respect. If you insult someone else's honey, that's one situation you won't be able to talk your way out of.

In short: avoid stupid people, stupid places or doing stupid things.

If all else fails, lift up the collar of your shirt and quietly say something like, 'Ten five, calling for back-up. It looks like we've got trouble here . . .' Then run for your life.

Behave in a Strip Club

When you enter a strip club, be prepared to part with some cash. Reckon on about £30 an hour for drinks and tips. Tip the bouncer on entering and you will get better seats.

Keep tipping the dancers – that's why they're up there showing their skin to you. If there's a dancer you keep checking out, then walk up and tip her. Don't just stare at the same woman with your tongue hanging out and your hands stuck in your pockets. If you are going to sit stageside, you'd better have lots of notes.

Look but don't touch, otherwise you will find yourself being dragged through the exit by two men without necks. And don't hit on a dancer. Just because she laughs at your jokes and takes off her clothes doesn't mean you're going to get lucky.

If you want a good seat near the front – ask and pay for it. Special booths or VIP lounges will cost you extra. Don't be afraid to ask about prices and what services are on offer. You may be able to afford more than you think.

Dress well and you'll get more attention from the dancers and more respect, so long as you keep tipping. If you dress like a bum, expect to be treated like one.

Don't bad-mouth one dancer to another – she won't see it as a compliment to her.

Get to know the DJ but don't pester him. He's usually well connected (often the dancers have to pay the DJ for their pitch). Offer to buy him a drink and tell him you like his music.

Don't assume you're better than the dancers. Not all of them are high-school drop outs with seven children. They may well be stripping to pay their way through college and be smarter and better educated than you.

Be friendly and treat the women with respect.

Don't get blind drunk or you'll do something you'll regret. Remember those two guys with no necks?

Be friendly and treat the women with respect. If you get yourself a table dance, talk to her – chances are she'll have some kiss-ass stories and be a good listener, too.

So now you know how to behave, sit back, soak up the atmosphere and admire the view. Eat, drink and show your appreciation with plenty of the green stuff.

KEEP TIPPING THE DANCERS — THAT'S WHY THEY'RE UP THERE SHOWING THEIR SKIN TO YOU.

Play Winning Poker

Whether you are a rookie or The Cincinnati Kid, more than any other game, poker requires a subtle understanding of other people. It's also about creative, logical, flexible thinking. And, above all, you must always keep your nerve while playing the percentages.

Rule #1:
Don't try to beat the other players; let them try to beat you.

Rule #2:
Think about Rule #1. If you don't grasp what this means, keep thinking until you do.

Rule #3:
Make sure you have at least fifty times the table limit.

Rule #4:
Know how good you are. If you've got a hand that rocks, it's just as easy for an opponent to read your excitement as your lame attempt to bluff by faking disinterest. Also, recognise the difference between playing badly, getting lucky and playing well.

Rule #5:
Choose your battles. Think long term, rather than trying to win every hand. It can be better to win nine small hands than one big pot.

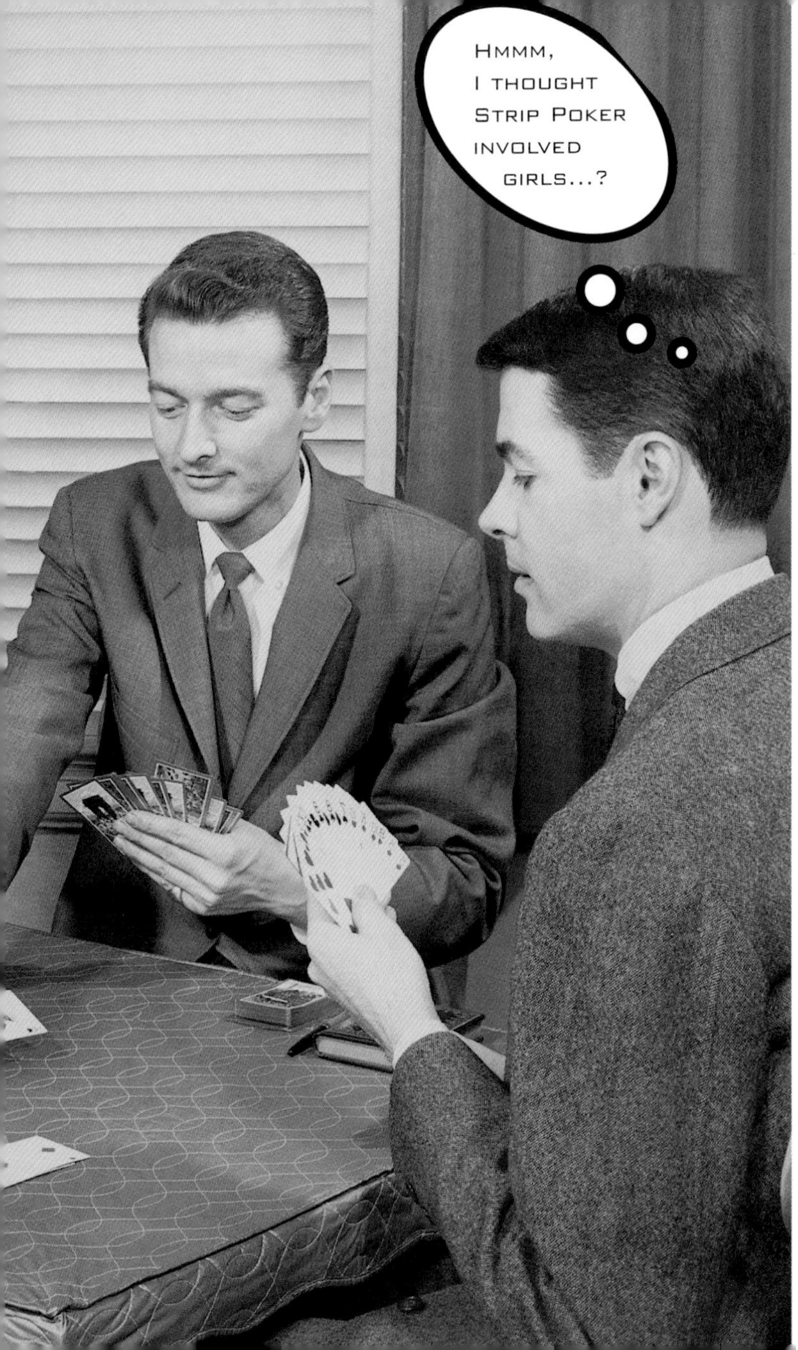
HMMM,
I THOUGHT
STRIP POKER
INVOLVED
GIRLS...?

Rule #6:

Try to play with those who are worse players than you. Obvious, but it's staggering how many people try to make a killing by taking on the big boys.

Rule #7:

Know the odds. There are 2,598,960 possible poker hands in a 52-card deck.

	Number of Possible Ways	Hand Can Be Dealt	Odds of Being Dealt in First 5 Cards
Royal Flush	4		1 in 649,740.00
Straight Flush	36		1 in 72,193.33
Four of a Kind	624		1 in 4,165.00
Full House	3,744		1 in 694.16
Flush	5,108		1 in 508.80
Straight	10,200		1 in 254.80
Three of a Kind	54,912		1 in 47.32
Two Pairs	123,552		1 in 21.03
One Pair	1,098,240		1 in 2.36
No Pair Hand	1,302,540		1 in 1.99

Rule #8:

If you've got nothing, get out. If you've got a great hand, make others pay dearly to see it.

Rule #9:

Bluff without a strategy and you'll regret it. Bluffing is not as important as understanding what makes your opponents tick. Remember that disguising your feelings crudely is a bigger give-away than showing them!

Rule #10:

Build your strategy from your first hand, rather than expecting a windfall when you change cards. The odds of improving your hand on the draw are about 50/50.

Rule #11:

You must expect to lose the pot unless you believe you have the best hand.

Rule #12:

People stare longer at better cards.

Rule #13:

Someone with a good hand is likely to feel more anxious than someone who is bluffing, since a bluffer can always fold. Look for how they handle that anxiety. How do they broadcast it and how do they try to conceal it?

Rule #14:

Mediocre players fall into patterns. Look out for repetitive behaviour.

Rule #15:

Don't assume that everyone thinks and feels like you. Have the flexibility to recognise you are dealing with individuals.

Cure a Hangover

If you want to prevent or 'cure' a hangover, you have first got to know what it is. That's easy, you say. It's when you 'hang over' the toilet seat with a carpet mouth, brain ache and the urgent need of a stomach transplant . . . but why do you feel like this after a heavy session?

Everyone knows that alcohol will make you dehydrated. (Didn't all those trips to the toilet the night before give you a clue? You were peeing out more than you drank. This is because alcohol inhibits your kidney's ability to absorb water, so the only place it can go is down the toilet.) But that's not the whole story. Your body will also be lacking in electrolytes (contained in body salts), vitamins, blood sugar and sleep, while it frantically tries to break down any remaining alcohol plus eliminating the nasty by-products (toxic chemicals like acetic acid and acetaldehyde).

The result is that your nervous system declares a state of emergency.

The night before
1. Do not drink on an empty stomach. Food helps to soak up the alcohol, so it doesn't all enter the bloodstream at the same time.
2. Broadly speaking, the lighter the drink, the less the hangover. All alcohol contains lots of nasty chemicals, but dark drinks have more (especially cheap red wine which has lots of

tyramine). If you drink white wine or vodka you should wake up feeling fresher than with the same number of units of red wine or beer.
3. Don't mix your drinks.
4. Have a soft drink for every alcoholic one. This will make you less drunk and will also keep you hydrated.

Before you sleep
1. Drink at least three pints of water. Every glass you drink now is worth two in the morning.
2. Eat a little food with a low glycemic index (one that releases its energy slowly), like protein (meat, fish, beans, pulses), fatty foods, fruit such as apples, peaches, oranges, plums (not bananas) or vegetables (except carrots and potato). Avoid sugary food and drinks.
3. Take a multivitamin. Some vitamins (like B) are soluble in water, so you will have peed them away during the evening.
4. Do not take a painkiller.

The morning after
1. Stay in bed.
2. Drink lots of water (even if you aren't thirsty).
3. Avoid caffeine drinks like coffee or colas, which will dehydrate you.
4. Don't drink any more alcohol.
5. Try to regulate your body temperature. When your body is under stress, its temperature rises, which is why a hangover is often accompanied by sweats.
6. Eat foods with a low glycemic index. Avoid sugary food and drinks. Eat little and often throughout the day.

Index